MOBILE

DEMCO

The Secret at
Octagon House

***Also by Jane Peart
in Large Print:***

A Perilous Bargain
Dreams of a Longing Heart
Homeward the Seeking Heart
Shadow of Fear
The House of Haunted Dreams
The Pattern
The Pledge
The Promise
The Risk of Loving
Thread of Suspicion
Web of Deception

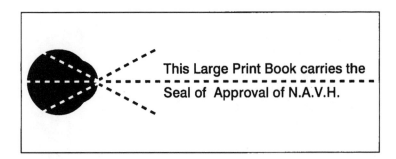

This Large Print Book carries the Seal of Approval of N.A.V.H.

The Secret at Octagon House

Jane Peart

Thorndike Press • Thorndike, Maine

Published in 2001 by arrangement with Natasha Kearn
Literary Agency, Inc.

Thorndike Press Large Print Candlelight Series.

The tree indicium is a trademark of Thorndike Press.

The text of this Large Print edition is unabridged.
Other aspects of the book may vary from the original edition.

Set in 16 pt. Plantin by Elena Picard.

Printed in the United States on permanent paper.

Library of Congress Cataloging-in-Publication Data

Peart, Jane.
    The secret at Octagon House / Jane Peart.
      p. cm.
    ISBN 0-7862-3114-9 (lg. print : hc : alk. paper)
    1. Large type books. I. Title.
PS3566.E238 S43 2001
813′.54—dc21   00-053236

The Secret at
Octagon House

Chapter One

Woodvale, Massachusetts
November 1898

The train from Boston was late, and as I stepped down onto the platform in the chill dampness of the early November evening, I shivered. I'd forgotten how cold it got in Woodvale at the onset of its long winters, forgotten how bleak the landscape was with the brooding forested hills.

There was no one to meet me. Not that I expected anyone. I had not sent word of the exact time of my arrival. In fact, it was only at the last minute that I had decided to accept Aunt Octavia's enigmatic invitation.

I had never meant to come back. Never wanted to — none of us had. Neither I nor my two Vale cousins, Elvira and Toby, with whom I'd grown up here. I could still hear Elvira's oft-repeated vow, "The day I walk out that door, I'll never set foot in this house again!"

I wondered whether she had kept that pledge, or if she, like myself, had been unable to resist Aunt Octavia. And Toby? Had he responded to this unexpected summons? Was it simply curiosity that had drawn me back?

Whatever it was, now, as I stood with the wind penetrating my thin coat, I doubted my wisdom in coming. Just being here brought back a flood of unhappy memories.

The few passengers who had left the train with me all seemed to have departed. The station house was unlighted and empty. I was alone on the deserted platform.

I turned up my collar and looked about. At the end of the platform I saw a shabby hack. Its driver was just backing up his horse to turn around, ready to leave. Hurrying toward him, waving my hand, I called breathlessly, "Are you free?"

The driver, slumped in the seat, lifted his head, swathed almost invisibly in a muffler. His bulbous, red nose and ruddy cheeks evidenced either a long wait in the cold or frequent trips to the tavern across from the station.

He pulled on the reins and, poking his face out of the wrapping of wool, hollered down at me, "Where to, miss?"

"To eighty Wyndom Place."

Was it my imagination, or did his hunched shoulders twitch as if startled when I gave the address? Giving himself a little shake, he climbed down from his perch. He rubbed his nose with the gnarled finger of one chapped hand and asked, "You mean *Octagon House?*"

"Yes, Octagon House," I repeated.

That was the name most Woodvale people called the Vale family mansion, the massive eight-sided structure that dominated the hillside just as the Vale lumber mill dominated the economy of the town. I'd forgotten that many people regarded the place with awe. We three cousins knew our schoolmates whispered behind our backs that it was haunted and called the acres of timberland that surrounded it Witch's Wood.

The driver seemed to hesitate.

I was tired, chilly, and feeling anxious and annoyed by his obvious reluctance. I frowned and asked, "Is anything wrong?"

"Well, miss, I was about to call it a day — it's a long ways up there. It'll be an extra fare."

"I'll pay whatever it is. I certainly can't walk," I snapped. I pointed to my suitcase, valise, and hatbox forlornly remaining on the empty platform. "There's my luggage. Will you please get it?"

The driver still stood, unmoving, staring at me with unabashed curiosity.

"Don't get many strangers coming here off the train. I mean, folks who don't live here."

I'd almost forgotten what it was like in a town as small as Woodvale. Six years had changed my perspective as well as my appearance. Of course this man, who regularly met the train, would notice someone he did not recognize.

But I felt no obligation to explain who I was or why I had come. Word would get around town soon enough, especially if Toby and Elvira arrived, too. Our being here would become common knowledge. There were no secrets in small towns; at least, not many.

As I watched the driver shuffle over to where I'd left my luggage, I realized there were many things about Woodvale that I'd also forgotten. Things I'd tried to forget. Like Jordan, I thought with the old bitterness. Jordan Barret, whom I'd loved with such passion, the man who had spoiled every other romantic relationship for me since.

In spite of myself I shuddered. Why did it hurt so much to remember Jordan? Was it just being back in Woodvale, where everything reminded me of him? What had I wanted to prove by coming back? That I was over him? A place shouldn't matter. Even a place filled with memories. Because memories are just that. Memories you can manage. Besides, Jordan had happened long ago. He was probably a brilliant surgeon in some big city hospital by now. Maybe even in Europe. I never expected to see Jordan again. Certainly not in Woodvale.

At last the driver came back with my luggage and finally opened the cab door for me so I could get in out of the cold. I settled myself on the worn leather seat of the musty interior. As he strapped my baggage to the back, the old cab wobbled and shook under his weight as he climbed back up on top. I heard him slap the reins, shout to his horse, and I felt the vehicle sway as we moved forward.

So, why *had* I come back? Curiosity, loneliness, whim? Some chance I could finally confront my childish ghosts? Of course, my aunt's letter had arrived at a difficult time in my life. My father's recent death had left me alone, vulnerable, facing an uncertain future with very little money or choice. Maybe it was simply a delaying tactic, a temporary reprieve before I had to make any definite decisions about my life.

11

As we jolted along the Woodvale streets illuminated by a few gas-lit street lamps, I looked out the window into the gathering fog and was reminded of another November evening much like this one, when I was nine years old and had just lost my mother a few months before. I did not fully understand why my young, grief-stricken father had sent me to stay with my mother's relatives at Octagon House. It was only to be for a short time. I ended up staying there nearly ten years.

As a child I first came to live at Octagon House. I was met by my aunt Octavia Vale, a tall, handsome woman, in a feathered hat and fur-trimmed cape. I remember we rode in silence, my strangely grim aunt and I, from the Woodvale train station. I was awed by her elegance as well as terrified by my new circumstances. When the carriage came to a stop, Aunt Octavia said, "Here we are at Octagon House, Juliette. Come along, your grandmother is waiting to see you."

I followed her in through etched-glass double doors, that were opened for us by a tall man, who I learned later was Marshall, the family butler. In the front hall, standing at the foot of the wide oak staircase, was a thin, freckled, red-haired girl about twelve, who eyed me suspiciously.

"Elvira, this is Juliette Madison," Aunt Octavia announced, nodding at me, as she stripped off her long kid gloves. Then she said, "This is your cousin Elvira Vale."

I had the immediate feeling that Elvira disliked me without even knowing me, that she resented my coming. I tried to smile at her, but I was too nervous.

Then Aunt Octavia walked across the hall, motioning me forward. "Come along, child," she said, and I obeyed.

I was ushered into an immense room with dark carved furniture. Over a black marble mantelpiece hung a huge, gold-framed mirror in which I saw myself reflected — a slight, sparrow like child with brown bangs nearly obscuring large, frightened gray eyes, a small face tense with anxiety.

Grandmother Vale must have once been a great beauty, but she was now quite wrinkled, although her silver hair was elaborately coiffed, and she was beautifully gowned in mauve velvet and heavy lace.

"Here she is, Stepmama," Aunt Octavia said, giving me a little shove between my shoulder blades toward the woman in the high-backed tapestried chair.

"So, this is *Juliette!*" my grandmother exclaimed in a high, petulant tone.

"Yes, this is *Juliette*." Even at my young

13

age I detected a scornful inflection in my aunt's voice.

"What an odd, romantic name to give a child!" declared my grandmother. "But so like Clemmy to do it," Octavia retorted with an edge of contempt. "Probably wanted to dramatize her elopement, comparing herself and that fool she married to Shakespeare's star-crossed lovers!"

Even all these many years later, remembering that remark of Aunt Octavia's, spoken so carelessly in front of a child still mourning the loss of a beloved mother, it still hurt and I winced. I could still hear Aunt Octavia's sarcastic tone. It was the same one she always used in reference to anything she did not like or understand.

My heartbeat matched the sound of the horse's hooves clomping on the wet cobblestone street as we started up the hill to Octagon House. I had a sudden urge to rap on the roof of the cab and tell the driver to turn around and take me back to the train station. Then I remembered there was probably no train out of Woodvale until morning. A moment later I heard the driver shout, "Whoa!" and we came to a shuddering stop. I knew we had arrived; it was too late to change my mind.

I peered out the mist-clouded window,

and there it was. Octagon House! Rising like some specter through swirling fog, its spiraling tiers surrounded by giant trees, it stood like a fortress at the end of a circular drive beyond the spiked iron fence.

When this house had been designed and built for my grandfather, Clement Vale, in the 1850s, only a few such eight-sided houses even existed. The octagonal shape was considered innovative architecturally as well as deeply symbolic. There was the strongly held belief at the time that the number eight was lucky. Octagon-shaped houses were supposed to bring good fortune, health, and happiness to those who lived in them. Tragically, that promise had not been fulfilled in the Vale family.

"Here you are, miss," the driver said, tugging open the cab door.

I got out and paid him. He had dumped my things on the ground beside me, not offering to carry them up to the circling porch. Standing motionless in front of the gate, I was hardly conscious of the rattling cab driving away.

I felt an eerie sense of déjà vu as I put out my hand to unlatch the gate. How strange it is to return to the place where you have lived as a child, I thought. It is like encountering the half-forgotten person you used to be.

Seeing the domed roof silhouetted brooding against the darkening winter sky, all the emotions of my first arrival descended upon me. Seeing the outline of the cupola at the top, I remembered vividly the time Elvira and Toby mischievously locked me in up there, then ran off, leaving me huddling in fright against one wall until Lutie, the cook, found me hours later.

I felt my mouth go dry, my throat tighten with apprehension, felt sweat gather in my palms underneath my gloves as a smothering panic gripped me. My cousins' childhood prank had resulted in a lifelong claustrophobic fear of heights and enclosed places. Even remembering the incident caused a reaction.

The conviction that it had been a terrible mistake to come back swept over me in a chilling wave. My hand froze on the latch of the gate. Yes, I'd been a fool to come. A fool to think I could exorcise the phantoms of the past that still haunted me.

I turned and was about to rush blindly through the fog swirling around me in wraithlike shreds, away from Octagon House. But suddenly the front door opened, and a shaft of light caught me in its beam. Then a familiar voice called, "Is that you, Julie?"

I recognized that voice at once. It was my cousin Elvira. Reluctantly I turned back. They knew I'd come. It was too late to escape whatever awaited me here at Octagon House.

Chapter Two

Even though there was no mistaking Elvira's shrill, demanding voice, the woman I saw standing at the edge of the veranda as I came up the steps, bore little resemblance to my once "ugly-duckling" cousin.

The light shining through the open door behind her created a flaming aura about her elaborately styled hair, and the "stringbean" young girl had become a willowy woman fashionably gowned in a gold and brown striped silk dress.

"Hurry up, let's get in out of this miserable night air," she urged. "Thank goodness you've come, Julie. I was afraid I was the only one idiotic enough to accept Aunt Octavia's invitation!" Elvira laughed nervously.

As I reached the top step she gave me a brief hug, enveloping me in the heavy scent of some exotic perfume. Then she took hold of my arm and led me into the house, saying, "Come on in out of this dreadful damp. I

18

can't wait to get a good look at you after all these years."

The minute I stepped inside I was struck by the feeling of the years rolling back. It all looked exactly as it had the first time I'd walked into Octagon House. Everything was the same: the dark oak paneling, the polished parqueted floor, and the gold-framed portrait of Grandfather Clement Vale, with his fierce blue eyes, thick red hair, and bushy beard, that still glared down from the most prominent place on the wall.

"Now, take off your coat and bonnet so I can see you!" ordered Elvira.

Amused, I did so, and while my cousin took inventory of *me,* I did the same to her. I was amazed to see the transformation she had undergone; gone was the carrotty hair, the freckles, the awkward adolescent I had last seen. Instead was a dramatically striking woman, beautifully dressed, with translucent skin and artfully arranged rich, auburn hair.

Her green eyes glittered like peridots as they narrowed in viewing me. "Well, Julie, you're all grown up, aren't you? And ever so pretty. Of course, your clothes are all wrong. But then, you never cared a fig for what you wore, did you?"

As usual, Elvira's comments were blunt. But because she had always been so self-

19

centered, they had an indifferent quality about them, so it was wise not to take them seriously. And I did not do so now even though it piqued me a little.

Tucking her hand through my arm, she started leading me toward the broad staircase. "Come along, we've been given our old rooms on the third floor, would you believe? I have so much to tell you, and of course, I want to hear all about you, too."

It was evident Elvira had things other than criticism of my apparel to discuss, but just then, out of the shadows, a figure appeared. It was the butler, Marshall, our aunt's "majordomo" at Octagon House.

"Marshall!" I exclaimed. "How nice to see you."

He bowed slightly and replied, "And you, Miss Julie. Miss Octavia will be pleased to know you've arrived. We weren't sure — that is, your telegram came only yesterday afternoon."

I thought I sensed a slight reproach in his tone, and I was quick to explain. "I wasn't sure, either. I mean, I had to make certain arrangements —" I stopped, no need to go into all my last-minute debate and misgivings about coming, I reminded myself. Instead I asked, "Where is my aunt? I'd like to say hello."

"Not seeing anyone," Elvira interjected. "At least, not yet. She's in her room resting, has been ever since I got here over two hours ago." Elvira sounded exasperated. "Sent word down she would see all three of us before dinner in the drawing room. I suppose that means Toby *is* coming, too."

Marshall darted a glance at Elvira in which I thought there was a flicker of distaste. But as if he saw me take note of it, his face quickly assumed its usual impassive expression, and he said, "We've had no definite word from Mr. Tobin."

"But he *is* coming?"

"We believe so, Miss Elvira —" He let the doubtful inference hang there.

Elvira looked at me and shrugged. We both remembered Toby's total disregard for being on time. In spite of repeated punishment for being late for meals and getting numerous tardy notices from teachers at school, Toby went on his own merry way, ignoring the high priority Aunt Octavia placed on punctuality.

"How *is* Aunt Octavia, Marshall?" I asked.

"Well, miss, she *is* getting on —" He paused tactfully.

"Miss Ingersoll is still here, Julie," Elvira interjected. "Imagine! She was Grandmother Vale's nurse, remember? Now she's taking care of Aunt Octavia. She's practically become an institution! It's *my* opinion she should be *in* one! She behaved quite irrationally when I wanted to see Aunt Octavia." Elvira gave a harsh laugh. She had always disliked Miss Ingersoll as much as she had Aunt Octavia, although she had made a secret of the latter.

The mention of the starchy, prim nurse made me wonder about the rest of the staff at Octagon House. Remembering the kindly housekeeper, I asked, "I suppose Mrs. Henshaw — ?"

"Retired," Marshall replied. "She left shortly after you young people did. She's living with her niece over in Perrysville."

"And Lutie?" I asked, not daring to hope my favorite of all the adults at Octagon House, the Danish cook, was still around.

"Yes, indeed, miss. Lutie's here just the same as always."

"Oh, good, I'm glad."

Elvira was tapping her foot impatiently, bored with my interrogation about the servants. "Come along, Julie, let's go up to our rooms so we can have some time together before dinner," urged Elvira.

"Elvira, I'm just going to pop into the kitchen and say hello to Lutie first. You go on; I'll be with you in a few minutes." Elvira looked peeved, but I didn't wait for her to give me some reasons not to go. I hurried down the long hallway toward the back of the house. Coming through the swinging door, I sniffed the wonderful smells that I always associated with this part of the house. In contrast to the cold atmosphere of the rest, it was always warm, welcoming and fragrant.

Pushing open the kitchen door, I saw the familiar broad back in a blue cotton dress, the crisp bow strings of the spotless pinafore apron over it, bending over the stove.

"Lutie!" I exclaimed.

She swiveled around, wooden spoon in hand, then let out a delighted cry. Lutie was happily unchanged: rosy-veined cheeks, eyes the color of bluebells circled with laugh lines, gray-brown hair pulled back into a knot with little wisps escaping out from under the white cap.

The next thing I knew I was being crushed against her soft bosom, immersed in the spicy scents of cinnamon and saffron and basil. As we hugged, all the best and sweetest childhood memories came flooding back. Of rainy days running home from school, flinging boots, bookbags, and raincoats in every direction to come out to the kitchen. There Lutie would be stirring a pan of cocoa, ready to pour it into mugs for us and serve it with thick slices of newly-baked bread spread with creamy butter.

"Miss Julie, little Miss Julie! How pretty you are!" declared Lutie. "You're the spittin' image of your mother! Wouldn't you say so Marshall?" she asked the butler, who had followed me into the kitchen, "Looks so much like Miss Clementine, don't she?"

I felt a lump in my throat. My mother, Clementine Vale, was never spoken of at Octagon House by either Grandmother Vale or Aunt Octavia. It was because of her elopement with my father, I knew. I'd often thought that maybe my looking like her had kept Grandmother Vale and Aunt Octavia from loving me.

The old longing for love instead of rejection suddenly rose up in me, and I just as quickly pushed it away. It didn't matter anymore. I certainly didn't care if Aunt Octavia loved me now.

I was, however, curious as to why she had invited me — us — here. Maybe Lutie knew. I'd been aware since childhood that nothing goes on "upstairs" that isn't known and discussed at length "downstairs." So when Lutie asked me if I'd like something hot "to take the chill off after that long cold ride from the train station," I sat down at the pine table, scrubbed white, while Lutie filled a cup with strong, fragrant coffee.

She poured a cup for herself and sat down opposite me. "Now, how's everything going? I've thought about you and the other two ever since you left here. Especially you. I want to hear all that's happened to you since." Her blue eyes twinkled merrily. "Likely there's a lucky young man in the picture."

I shook my head. "I'm afraid not, Lutie."

"What?" she scoffed. "Pretty as you are and no beau?" Her rosy cheeks dimpled and she said, "Well, then, we'll just have to take a look into the teacups."

"Oh, Lutie, remember how we used to beg you to tell our fortunes?"

"I do, indeed, you and that Miss Elvira! Oh, my! Once *she* got something into her head, there was no peace till I gave in." Lutie shook her head and chuckled. Then, with a sly look, she asked, "So, you've already seen Miss Elvira, have you?"

I nodded. Lutie lifted her plump chin and said loftily, "My, but she's come back a fine lady! Not that I'm too surprised. She always had a way of putting on airs even as a girl, remember? Loved to dress up! Do you remember the time she borrowed your aunt's fox fur when Miss Octavia was out one afternoon? What a fuss there'd have been if your aunt had discovered it. Well, now she has furs of her own and to spare, from the looks of it." Lutie lowered her voice, leaned closer, and said, "Married to some high and mighty muckety-muck, to hear her tell it. Come sweeping in with eight pieces of luggage, all fine leather, with her initials in gold on them. Wanted to see Miss Octavia right away the minute she come, but Miss Ingersoll insisted she wasn't to be disturbed." Lutie made a clucking sound. "She and Miss Ingersoll had a fine howdy-do right there and then. But nobody gets past *her*. We call her the 'guard dog' down here, don't we, Marshall?" Lutie turned her head to get Marshall's agreement, but somewhere in the middle of all this, Marshall had quietly disappeared.

"I was sorry to hear about your father's death, Miss Julie. I thought he was such a quiet, pleasant fellow when he first came courting Clemmy — Miss Clementine. Anyone could see how in love they were, but the Vales were against it — especially Miss Octavia —" Lutie broke off, flushing and biting her lip.

I had the distinct feeling Lutie was about to say more then decided not to, which increased the uneasy feeling I had had from the minute I had stepped across the threshold. Octagon House was a place of shadows and secrets, hidden motives, unexplained circumstances. I'd felt it as a child and I still felt it now. Again, I wished I hadn't come back.

As if she had read my mind, Lutie put a comforting hand over mine and said, "I'm sorry, Miss Julie. I shouldn't have brought up all the old hurts. I'm so glad to see you, dearie, I'm glad you come back." Then Lutie gave me a quick, strange look and added, "I hope you won't be sorry you did."

At Lutie's words an icy finger of apprehension trailed down my spine. In spite of her cheerful smile as I left, what she said lingered uneasily in my mind.

Chapter Three

As I left the kitchen and passed through the dining room, Marshall was standing at a massive mahogany sideboard pouring wine into cut-glass decanters. He looked at me and said, "I'll carry your bags up to your room now, Miss Julie. It's a long climb to the third floor. Miss Octavia gave orders you were to have your old rooms during your visit."

The entire third floor had belonged to Elvira, Toby, and me when we lived here as children. On the second floor were the rooms of the adults of the household, Grandmother Vale's suite, Aunt Octavia's and Uncle Victor's wings, all pie-shaped as dictated by the singular structure of Octagon House. Above us, on the top floor, were the servants' quarters, the attic, and the cupola.

Marshall led the way out to the front hall. He picked up my suitcase and valise, then I took my hatbox and followed him up the two flights of stairs and down to the end of the long corridor. He opened the door to my old room and set down my bags.

"Dinner will be at eight, Miss Julie. Miss Octavia requested that you all meet in the drawing room at seven-thirty."

After he left, I stood gazing around the room I'd occupied as a child. Here it seemed that time had stood still.

Although far neater than when I had lived in it, essentially everything was the same. The high brass bed with a white crocheted spread, a quilt folded at the bottom. The wallpaper, faded now, still had its trellis of climbing roses. The fishnet curtains hung stiffly at two tall windows. Wedged between them was the slant-topped desk where I used to do my homework; on it the oil lamp with its green glass globe.

Slowly I circled the room, remembering the girl who had gone through all the stages of growing up here, studying, sleeping, getting up, pouting, crying, giggling, plotting all sorts of mischief with Elvira, reading contraband novels, dreaming of falling in love — Unwanted, the thought of Jordan thrust itself into my consciousness. In this room I'd written those first secret love letters, dreaming my romantic dreams, hoping my — in the end, foolish — hopes . . .

My nostalgic reminiscences were suddenly broken into by a knock on my door, and a second later it was flung open and Elvira burst into the room.

"What on earth kept you?" she demanded. "I've been waiting ages for you to come up so we could talk!"

"I was with Lutie," I began, "and I was going to unpack —"

"Well, go ahead. I won't bother you. I'll just perch on the end of the bed, and we can have our chat!" Elvira settled herself there, gathering around her the yards of pale green velvet dressing gown adrift with swirls of fluted chiffon. "Julie, can you *believe* it, the two of us, actually back here at Octagon House? Never in my wildest dreams would I have imagined I'd *ever* come back." She tossed her loosened flame-colored hair and shook her head. "I was so glad to be gone from here. And of course, my life has been so marvelous ever since! You knew my mother remarried, of course? A *very wealthy* man. She left the stage then, and he took us to Europe. He was quite a bit older than she was, but such an old dear. Doted on me. He was a widower with no other children, so he treated me as if I were his own daughter. What a change after living here and being treated like an *orphan — a poor relation!*"

I began putting away my things. Out of

30

habit I found myself using the same bureau drawers I always had: shirtwaists and camisoles in the middle drawers, petticoats laid flat on the bottom, stockings and gloves in the smaller top ones.

While I unpacked, Elvira chatted nonstop about her travels, how she had met Drew Breckenridge while she was with her parents on the Riviera, her whirlwind romance and marriage, and the hectic social life they now lived in New York. Midstream, Elvira halted. Focusing her direct gaze upon me, she asked, "Julie, why do you think Aunt Octavia asked us all to come back?"

"I have no idea," I answered truthfully, thinking what was just as puzzling was why *we* had accepted the invitation.

"It couldn't have been simply a senile whim," Elvira continued, frowning, "because I am quite sure Aunt Octavia is far from senile. Her letter sounded just as concise and clear-minded as ever. But I'm still baffled. She certainly cared little enough for us when we were children. And I've never heard a word from her since I left." Elvira's green eyes darkened as she asked, "Have *you?*"

I shook my head.

"I wonder if *Toby* — I think he was always her favorite of the three of us, don't you?"

31

Before I could venture an opinion, a discreet tap sounded on the door. It was Marshall.

"Excuse me, miss, I wondered if you are ready for me to take your luggage up to the attic?"

"Yes, thank you, Marshall. I've finished unpacking," I replied.

"Mine are in the hall, Marshall," Elvira told him offhandedly.

"Yes, madam, I got them," Marshall said and, after picking up my two, went silently out of the room.

Elvira made a face. "Same old sphinx, isn't he? Never could tell what he was thinking. Sort of gives me the creeps, always has."

I checked my fob watch pinned to my blouse. It was after six. Following my glance, Elvira asked what time it was. When I told her, she jumped off the bed.

"Uh-oh, we'd both better get dressed. I suppose Aunt Octavia still expects promptness, and I don't want to start off on the wrong foot with the old ogre." Elvira smiled wickedly and started to the door. "And since Marshall made the point that dinner would be a formal affair, I want to dazzle her with one of my Paris gowns." Hand on the doorknob, she turned back to me, saying severely, "You, too, Julie. I hope you have something suitable to wear. For heaven's sake, don't come down dressed like a schoolmarm." With that final annoying dig she spun out of the room.

I bristled a little, then shrugged. I should be used to Elvira's critical comments. I'd certainly endured enough of them when we were both girls here. Elvira had always been hopelessly blunt, and in spite of her veneer of social graces, time had not improved Elvira's tact.

I opened the armoire to look over the dresses I'd hung there. What would I wear for our first dinner back at Octagon House? Maybe there was nothing in my meager wardrobe Elvira would consider "suitable." Actually Elvira's warning was not too far off the mark. I smiled ruefully. All of them seemed dreadfully "schoolmarmish."

Although I never actually taught school, I *had* attended the Merrivale Teachers College for two years. When I went to live with my father, a professor in a small Midwestern college, I got a job as a researcher to the history professor.

It didn't take me long to make my decision between two possible choices: a black taffeta and a royal blue wool. The black reminded me of the last time I'd worn it, at my father's funeral, so I quickly chose the blue one.

As I dressed I thought about Elvira. Beneath the superficial sophistication I sensed the old insecurities still lurked, and under the surface gaiety of the glittering life she led was a kind of emptiness.

I brushed my dark hair, thankful that it was naturally curly and thick enough to sweep it up into the popular Gibson girl pompadour without a false "rat." Before going downstairs, I gave myself a final check in the mirror, noting with satisfaction that even though I was too thin to claim the fashionable hourglass figure, my dress, with its long, fitted bodice and leg-o'-mutton sleeves, was in style, its color becoming. Then something weird happened.

I seemed to hear Aunt Octavia making the remark I'd overheard often as a child: "*She hasn't Clemmy's beauty and never shall.*" I hadn't thought of that for years. Maybe I'd blocked it out. Now, in an instant, I was that little girl again, feeling unloved, unaccepted. Involuntarily I shuddered. "I should *never* have come back here," I told my reflection.

Then I lifted my chin defiantly. I *wasn't* that vulnerable child anymore! I'd left all that behind me. I'd kept house for my father, I'd had a good education and now held a responsible job, I'd been told I was attractive —

"Fool!" I accused my image and turned away. I was not going to let echoes of old hurts bother me.

In spite of my bravado I was trembling. I walked over to the window and looked out. It was dark now. Through the trees surrounding the house I could see the dim glow of a few street lamps on the road, and beyond, in the distance, the lights of Woodvale.

As I stood at the window, I saw a buggy turn in the gates and come up the drive and under the porte cochere at the side of the house.

Toby! I thought. It must be Toby arriving!

I remembered what an endearing little boy he had been when, newly orphaned, he first came to Octagon House. Elvira and I had taken him under our wing immediately. During our years together here the three of us became inseparable.

Suddenly I couldn't wait to see him. Eagerly I rushed out the bedroom door and into the hall. I ran down the steps from the third floor and along the second-floor corridor to start down the next flight to the lower hall. But as I did I was dealt a shocking blow.

Instead of Toby I came face-to-face with the man who had broken my heart.

Chapter Four

Jordan Barret!

He was standing with Aunt Octavia's nurse, Flora Ingersoll, at the top of the steps. Before I realized who it was, before I could turn and run, they both saw me. Miss Ingersoll said coolly, "Oh, I did not know you had come yet."

Jordon said nothing; he just stared at me.

If it is possible for a heart to stand still, mine did. Then it began to pound wildly. I could not seem to draw a deep breath. I actually thought I might faint.

Seeing Jordan again, all my old feelings for him sprang to tingling awareness. After all the years of trying to forget him, it was devastating to find the door I had closed so firmly on the past was reopening. Our eyes locked in what seemed an endless moment. He did not speak and I could not.

Speechless though I was, my eyes absorbed the man Jordan had become. The tall, lanky body had become lean, broad-shouldered. His boyish features had matured and sharpened into a face of strength and character. The mouth that had once kissed mine with youthful ardor was now straight and stern. And there were lines between the heavy eyebrows and around the eyes. But the look in those eyes chilled me. Where once his eyes had looked at me with warm, loving tenderness, they were now regarding me as coldly as a winter sea.

Miss Ingersoll's clipped voice jolted me out of my shocked trance. "This is your aunt's physician, Dr. Barret. This is Miss Madison, one of Miss Vale's nieces."

"Miss Madison." Jordan inclined his head with a wry smile as if enjoying the irony of our being introduced.

Unconscious of the terrible tension between us, Miss Ingersoll complained, "I was just telling Dr. Barret, I don't approve of this at all — this reunion. Your aunt has been agitated for weeks — too much excitement is very bad for her. But there was no dissuading her." Miss Ingersoll's lips pursed.

"As I told you, Nurse, her condition remains unchanged, no better, no worse," Jordan commented dryly. "I've added a mild sedative to her present medication, which should keep her from becoming over-stimulated by this change in her routine." Then he turned to me. "She's not used to a lot of company, activity, conversation. In fact, Miss Vale has lived rather as a recluse these past years. I would caution you and your cousins not to do or say anything that would disturb her — emotionally or —" He paused, then said to Miss Ingersoll, "I suggest you take precautions that she doesn't get overtired." He turned back to me and said with special emphasis, "Fatigue seems to precipitate an attack of pain. Stress of any sort should be avoided. We've learned that stress is a factor in the type of arthritis your aunt suffers from."

I kept standing there, seeing no way to go past them. I felt sick at heart but unable to move.

Then Jordan once again directed himself to the nurse. "Well, then, I'll be on my way, Miss Ingersoll. As usual, if you should have need of me, you have only to send for me." Then, turning an indifferent glance on me, he gave a brief nod and said, "I trust you will enjoy your stay at Octagon House, Miss Madison."

With that he proceeded down the stairway. From where I stood, I watched as Marshall took his medical bag, helped him into a caped tweed coat, then handed him his hat. Before putting it on, Jordan seemed to hesitate, then turned and looked back up to the landing where I was. Quickly I took a step back. The next thing I heard was the slam of the front door.

Once again Miss Ingersoll's tone was curt. "I told Miss Octavia it was a mistake inviting you three back here. I begged her to reconsider the whole idea of it! But it did no good. And now you're here, you and that other one. Do you know *she* made a scene, insisting on seeing your aunt the minute she walked in this house as if she owned it?"

In amazement I saw Miss Ingersoll had lost the professional manner she had maintained in Jordan's presence. Her face was mottled with red blotches. Eyes flashing, voice shaking, she said, "Well, I want to make one thing crystal clear, Miss Madison, and you can relay this information to your cousin. *I* am in charge of your aunt's health and welfare, and I will *not* have that authority brooked! If any one of you does anything to cause her to become upset, I'll hold you responsible for the consequences."

After delivering that ultimatum, Miss Ingersoll brushed past me and marched down the hall toward Aunt Octavia's wing of the house.

Shaken by both encounters, I went downstairs, noticing that Marshall still stood by the front door. He looked at me impassively as I went by him, yet I knew he could not have helped hearing Miss Ingersoll's words.

In the drawing room a fire was lighted in the black marble fireplace, and the ruby-glass globed lamps were lighted, casting a jewel-like glow over the room. Still gripped by the shock of seeing Jordan again, I moved stiffly over to the velvet sofa and sat down. In spite of the warmth from the fire, I felt cold and painfully depressed.

In all the times I'd fantasized about meeting Jordan again, it had never been like this. I had imagined, somehow, that all the misunderstanding would be explained, the questions answered, the wounds healed. I'd never thought it would be so passionless, so — cold! No, never like this! I could hardly believe what I'd seen in Jordan's eyes. Dislike, disdain — contempt?

I had no time to agonize over the mortifying scene with Jordan or the disturbing one with Aunt Octavia's nurse that had followed, because I heard Elvira's voice in the hall speaking to Marshall. Quickly I tried to regain my composure. A minute later she swept into the room with a swish of taffeta and a whisper of her exotic perfume.

Elvira looked stunning in an apple-green

dinner gown with tiers of fluted ruffles that rippled to the floor, ending in a short train. Her once unmanageable red hair was beautifully coiffed and her complexion artfully perfect. As she held out her long hands to the fire's warmth, I saw the brilliance of a large emerald ring. Eyes sparkling with excitement, she demanded, "Do you know who just left? Jordan Barret. Marshall told me he's now Aunt Octavia's physician. Took over his uncle's practice a few years ago. Fancy that, Jordan a doctor. I remember he was the handsomest fellow in high school when he lived here. Do you?" Then Elvira shot me a curious glance and asked, "Didn't *you* have some sort of crush — ?"

I braced myself for her question but was rescued from what it was going to be by the sound of footsteps and voices approaching from the hall. We both looked in that direction as Aunt Octavia, accompanied by Miss Ingersoll, entered the drawing room.

Automatically I rose to my feet at my aunt's entrance. Although leaning on a cane and on the arm of her nurse, Aunt Octavia held herself as regally as her crippling disease would allow. She was dressed like a queen, in a dinner gown of rich gold panne velvet. Exquisite lace at the neck and falling over the wrists concealed the wrinkled neck and swollen hands, deformed by the arthritis. Her aristocratic face still bore traces of the youthful attractiveness we had seen in old photographs of her. Her hair was startlingly orange above her pale, deeply lined face. Her eyes, dark and bright as cut onyx, made a quick reconnaissance of the room, darting between Elvira and me.

Although my immediate impression was that Aunt Octavia had aged remarkably well, I had the feeling that she was a troubled, deeply unhappy woman and that those emotions had etched themselves indelibly on her face.

She did not speak until Miss Ingersoll had helped her lower herself into a high-backed chair by the fireplace and adjusted a footstool on which to place her satin-slippered feet. Both Elvira and I waited silently like courtiers attending royalty. When she was seated, she looked directly at me, saying, "Well, Juliette."

I went over to her, all at once feeling very young and uncertain. "It's good to see you looking so well, Aunt Octavia. Thank you for inviting me and sending me the train ticket to come." She waved her hand as if shooing away a tiresome fly.

"Never mind that. You're here. And Elvira" — she gave Elvira an inscrutable glance — "who made her presence known the minute she came through the door! And Toby, I understand, is on his way. But who knows when he'll show up?" She frowned and said testily, "Victor should be here. Why my brother is always late I do not understand. He was brought up the same as I, taught that to keep others waiting was a discourtesy. Ingersoll, go upstairs and knock at his door, see what's delaying him."

Miss Ingersoll scurried out of the room, passing Marshall on his way in, bearing a tray with a decanter and glasses.

"Ah, the sherry. Put it down here, Marshall." Aunt Octavia indicated the low, pink marble-topped table in front of her. "This is a fine Spanish sherry I have been saving for some *special* occasion — but *this* one will have to suffice, I suppose. It's an *unusual* occasion anyway. With all of us gathered *en famille*, eh?" She gave a brief little laugh that had no mirth in it.

Elvira slipped me a surreptitious glance, then swiftly assuming a gracious demeanor, suggested, "Would you like me to pour, Aunt Octavia?"

Elvira seemed anxious to impress our aunt with her refined new persona, far removed from the gauche young girl she had been. I thought I saw a sly smile twitch Aunt

Octavia's mouth as if she were on to Elvira's game, but all she said was, "Yes, go ahead. We shan't wait for either of them."

As Elvira filled the fragile, delicate-stemmed wineglasses, she began talking animatedly about her recent trip to the south of France. She pointedly dropped names of most of the reigning crowned heads of Europe vacationing there, implying she had hob-nobbed with them.

I tried to concentrate on what Elvira was saying, but instead of impressing me, it bored me. I found my thoughts drifting back to the upsetting meeting with Jordan. Determinedly I thrust them away. Later, when I was in my room alone, I would deal with it, I told myself.

Consciously I distracted myself by study-ing my surroundings. We had seldom been allowed to come in the drawing room as children. Now, as my eyes roamed about, I thought that it looked exactly the same as the day Aunt Octavia had ushered me in here to meet Grandmother Vale.

Its ornately carved and curved rosewood furniture, upholstered in dark green velvet, all set in the same places. The heavy drap-eries with their scalloped valances and tas-seled tie-backs, the gold ormolu clock on the mantelpiece, and over it, the baroque framed mirror reflecting us all like a scene in a play . . . Yes, it was all unchanged, I thought — and yet, not quite. Something seemed to be missing, but I could not figure out what was different.

According to Uncle Victor, in the old days Octagon House was famous for entertaining, and this room had been the scene of many gala parties. Our aunt's younger brother, and our parents' older half brother, was as different from his sister as it was imaginable. When we lived here as children, he was often away traveling, but when he was at home, I remembered him as being a charming gentleman, with a cheerful disposition and gracious manners. His rather absentminded ways irritated Aunt Octavia, but we children thought them vastly amusing. We loved hearing the interesting stories of his travels, and he knew many fascinating things. It was Uncle Victor who told me the history of Octagon House.

From him I discovered how rare octagon-constructed houses were. When Grandfather Clement Vale had this one built, it caused quite a flurry. It was built on four levels. The main rooms were square with wedge-shaped rooms in between to form the outer octagon shape. A circular staircase, cantilevered in the center, mounted on all levels. On the top floor the glass-enclosed cupola was a place Grandfather Vale could use his telescope, indulging his hobby of astronomy.

For its day the house was a marvel of advanced engineering. The outside walls of the house were surrounded by a colonnaded porch. The walls, each over a foot thick, had vents placed to provide a continuous circulation of fresh air from outside, while their thickness insulated the house from summer heat. It also had water for the modern bathrooms run through pipes from a cistern in the basement.

My wandering thoughts were retracted from the past by Aunt Octavia's sharp exclamation. "Well, it's about time!"

I turned to see Uncle Victor, his cravat and coattails flying, come puffing into the room.

"My dear girls!" he greeted Elvira and me, his rosy face wreathed in a broad smile. "How very nice to see you both again." Then, turning to his sister, he apologized, "Very sorry, Octavia, not to be on hand earlier to help you welcome Julie and Elvira here on their first evening. But I was at the library in town and became involved in an extremely interesting piece of historical data that Martha — I mean, Miss MacAndrews, the librarian, found for me. Research for my book, you know. . . ." He nodded to us as if for confirmation.

Elvira and I exchanged a look. For as long as we could remember, Uncle Victor had been working on "his book," a proposed volume on Woodvale and Vale family history.

"Yes, well, Victor, don't bore us with all that *tonight*," Octavia cut in curtly. "It's nearly eight, and you *know* I always have dinner served on the dot as Father did. So if you want a sherry beforehand, drink up."

"Ah, yes, well . . ." Uncle Victor stammered, abashed by Octavia's reprimand, and meekly helped himself to a glass of sherry.

Aunt Octavia's unnecessary rudeness angered me. I glanced at her. *She* hadn't changed. She still was as sharp-tongued and insensitive as ever. At once I decided I would try to spend some time with Uncle Victor while I was here.

The clock began to chime, and at a signal from Aunt Octavia we all started for the dining room, where the handsomely appointed table was set for five. At each end stood eight-branched silver candelabra, and the flames from the tall tapers gleamed on the white octagon-shaped china flanked by the heavily engraved sterling service and etched crystal goblets.

We had just been seated when the sound of the metal doorbell being twisted echoed stridently through the house.

Aunt Octavia's eyebrows lifted and her lips twitched in a travesty of a smile as she said, "Toby, no doubt!"

Chapter Five

We heard voices in the hall and turned expectantly toward the dining room door. I felt a nervousness I could not explain. I hoped Toby was returning as a conquering hero, yet for some reason I felt an indefinable anxiety.

A moment later there he was standing in the doorway, his arms flung out in greeting, "Aunt Octavia!"

He went over to her and, leaning down, placed his cheek against hers. At the same time his eyes moved around the table and acknowledged each of us.

"Elvira! Julie! My beautiful cousins! And Uncle Victor."

Uncle Victor got to his feet and pumped Toby's hand vigorously. "Capital to see you, my boy!"

Happy as I was that Toby had come, as I watched him I had the disturbing impression that Toby was acting a part and that he was playing it to the hilt.

Early on Aunt Octavia had recognized

49

that Toby was musical and saw to it that he took piano lessons. I knew that he had been accepted at a music conservatory the year after he graduated from the boys' boarding-school where Aunt Octavia had sent him at twelve. By that time I had left Octagon House and had eventually lost contact with Toby. I assumed he must now be pursuing a musical career.

He certainly looked the way a musician is supposed to, I thought. His russet-red hair was a little too long, curling at the neck; he wore a velvet jacket and a flowing silk tie under a Byron-collared shirt.

Toby was charmingly apologetic about his late arrival. He began a long, involved story about a rock slide en route delaying his train several hours until the tracks were cleared.

"Well, be that as it may, sit down, Toby," Aunt Octavia interrupted. "Our soup will be stone cold, and Lutie will be upset if the rest of the meal is held."

When Toby took his seat opposite me, I had a chance to observe my cousin at closer range. He was as handsome a man as he had been as a child. But he was too thin. Watching how hungrily he dived into the main course, I could not help wonder if Toby ate regularly. However, there was something that troubled me more. What made someone twenty look closer to thirty?

I also noticed that Toby's jacket needed pressing, that the lapels and cuffs were worn, the elbows were shiny, and the edges of his shirt collar were frayed. I was sure his general "down-at-the-heels" look had not escaped Aunt Octavia's eagle eyes.

Just then Toby glanced over at me. His eyes had the same haunted look he'd had as a little boy when he had first been brought to Octagon House by strangers to live with strangers. They still held an unfulfilled need. Stricken to the heart, I looked away, feeling helpless.

Dinner began to seem endless. Dessert, carmelized custard, one of Lutie's specialties, was served, but all I could manage was one spoonful. My appetite had been ruined by the evening's succession of traumatic events: seeing Jordan earlier, followed by the abrasive encounter with Miss Ingersoll and now this dismaying intuitive concern about Toby.

Finally the dessert dishes were taken away, and Aunt Octavia announced, "We'll have our coffee in the drawing room." With obvious difficulty she started to rise, and Elvira nearly knocked over her own chair as she rushed to assist her. Aunt Octavia accepted her help but with poor grace, and I could tell my aunt deeply resented her infirmity. Toby gallantly took her other arm, and the two of them escorted her across the hall. I followed behind them with Uncle Victor.

We were all a little strange with one another after so many years, and conversation was strained as we sipped our coffee from tiny demitasse cups. At one point Aunt Octavia spoke directly to Toby. "You are probably tired from your long and eventful trip, Tobin, but perhaps tomorrow night, when you're rested, you will favor us with a selection or two." She indicated the baby grand piano in the corner. I thought I saw Toby wince slightly. But he nodded and murmured compliance.

"You were enormously talented as a child, your teacher told me. Quite unusual in a child your age when you started lessons," Aunt Octavia went on. "I hope with maturity and training that talent has been fulfilled. It is important to keep studying, improving, and achieving in any field, but especially in music. Don't you agree?"

Toby answered in such a low voice I had to lean forward to hear his reply. It was something about studying Pythagorean music for the last year or so. I didn't recognize the term and automatically glanced at

Elvira to see if she did. But she was looking blankly at Toby, so I knew she did not understand, either.

There seemed no possible comment on this, and another awkward silence fell. Finally Aunt Octavia said, "I assume what is foremost in all of your minds is why I asked you to come back to Octagon House and what my reasons were for bringing you all together. But since it is now so late, and I find I tire easily these days, I am going to retire. We'll postpone our discussion until tomorrow." She reached for the tapestry bellpull hanging from the wall beside her and yanked it.

Miss Ingersoll materialized so quickly I had the feeling she must have been just outside the drawing room door and listening to everything. There was something about the woman that set my teeth on edge. She helped Aunt Octavia to her feet, and they started moving haltingly across the room. At the door our aunt drew herself up and, turning back toward us, made a provocative statement. "I assure all of you that eventually you will feel coming here was worthwhile no matter what personal inconvenience it may have caused."

Her enigmatic exit line dangled in the silent room after her departure. After a moment Uncle Victor rose and, pleading work to do on his book, excused himself. Before leaving, with his old-fashioned courtesy, he assured each of us how pleased he was to see us again.

After he left, Elvira stood up, stifling a yawn and said, "Sorry, you two, I'd adore staying up till all hours catching up on everything, but I simply cannot keep my eyes open a minute longer. So I'm forced to say *bon nuit*." She stretched languidly and then blew a kiss to both of us before disappearing.

I was left alone with Toby. "Well, Julie, it looks like it's you and me holding the fort." He smiled at me and suggested, "Let's have a nightcap." The before-dinner sherry was still on the table, and he removed the top of the decanter, filled two glasses, and handed one to me.

"Here's to a grand and glorious family reunion." He lifted his glass in a toast. "Whatever the reason for it."

I raised my glass, too.

"Who would have ever thought we'd find ourselves back here after all this time. And who would have thought my cousin Julie would turn out to be such a beauty?"

I blushed and laughed a little self-consciously. It was easy to see why Lutie

54

used to say, "That Toby could charm the bugs off a potato vine." He had lost none of that irresistible charm, I thought. But even as I acknowledged this, out of the past came the picture of the day I had come home from school and found that little boy standing in the downstairs hall, looking at me with those same eyes, begging "love me, be my friend." There was something still of that lost, lonely child in this handsome, charming man. Too handsome, too charming?

He was regarding me over the rim of his glass, and I braced myself for what I knew was coming.

"How is it you're not — ?"

"Don't ask!" I warned. "If you want to play Twenty Questions, Toby, would you please tell me what in the world Pythagorean music is anyway?"

A slow grin started at the corners of his mouth and rose into mischievous eyes. Again I was reminded of the little boy as he laughed and said, "Well, actually it's just a theory I came across once when I was reading about the occult. It was described as the alchemy of music, the study of what combinations of tones evoke what emotions." He shrugged indifferently. "That's all I know about it. But you know how it is when Aunt Octavia asks you something point blank; you've got to come up with something before she pins you to the wall!"

Same old Toby, I thought. Always ready with the easy excuse, the appropriate alibi. I hoped it hadn't become a habit in his adult life.

Toby drained his glass then asked, "Ready for another?"

"No, thanks, Toby. It's been a long day; I think I'll call it a night." I set down my glass as he was refilling his. Carrying it, he walked with me out into the hall.

"What kind of card do you suppose Aunt Octavia is going to pull out of her sleeve tomorrow? Think she's going to show her hand? Trump everyone's ace? Aren't you curious as to why she's called us all back here?" He spoke with such elaborate casualness, I had the uneasy feeling it was terribly important to him.

"You sound like a gambler, Toby."

"Aren't we all? Why did *you* come, Julie?"

"I'm still trying to figure that out," I said.

"In the end I guess we all play the hand we're dealt." He smiled, but his eyes were serious. Then surprisingly he leaned over and kissed my cheek. "It really is good to see you, Julie. You always were my favorite."

That touched me. I reached out and patted his shoulder. Then we said good night, and I went upstairs. At the landing I turned and looked back down and saw Toby heading toward the drawing room. There was something about the way his shoulders were hunched that tugged my heart. I hoped I was wrong about my cousin and that things had gone well in his life.

I paused for a second as I went by Elvira's door. But there was no light underneath and no sound from within, so I assumed she was sound asleep.

Sleep did not come so easily for me.

I was physically exhausted and emotionally drained. The day had been full of unexpected shocks. Seeing Jordan had been the worst, of course. I thought I'd gotten over him. But old loves die hard, they say. Maybe first loves die even harder. And Jordan Barret was my first love.

Of course, I had known Jordan when he attended Woodvale High School, but three years ahead of me. As a lowly freshman I had had a terrible crush on the handsome senior. After graduation Jordan had gone away to the university, then to medical school. I didn't see him again until I came home from my first year at Merrivale Teachers College for Christmas vacation.

There had been snow, then a hard freeze, and the pond in Woodvale Park was covered with thick, solid ice. The first day it was declared safe for skating, Toby and I tramped through the woods over to the park. Elvira hated cold like a cat and was curled up with a romance novel.

At the pond Toby wasted no time and was out on the ice in a flash. I was out of practice and entered from the side more cautiously. I was taking it slowly, circling around the rim close to the rail, when suddenly someone skated up alongside and spun to a stop in front of me, scattering flecks of ice.

"Julie Madison, isn't it? Remember me, Jordan Barret?"

I looked up into a windburned face, sparkling blue eyes, and a wonderful smile. *Remember* him, I thought? I'd never forgotten him. "Sure," I'd managed to say.

Before I knew it, we were skating together, talking as if we'd always been friends. He was spending the holidays with his uncle, Dr. Hugh Barret, he told me. I don't know how many times we circled the pond before Jordan asked if I'd like to get some hot chocolate.

There was a small refreshment stand, usually just open in the summertime to sell soda and ice cream cones, but they'd reopened it for this special skating season. We sat on one of the benches drinking our cocoa and talked some more. Afterward we went back on the pond, this time arm in arm. Jordan even started teaching me to skate backward.

Soon, too soon for me, long, purple shadows were crisscrossing the ice, and the sun was fast disappearing. Toby had met up with some of his friends and was getting ready to leave when Jordan and I finally quit skating.

Kneeling down in front of me, unlacing my skates, Jordan said, "I'll walk you home."

I remember how unbelievably happy I was as we walked along the snowy paths up the hill to Octagon House. When we reached the high, spiked iron fence enclosing the grounds, Jordan looked up at the house and said off-handedly, "I guess you know some people in Woodvale are scared to death of this place. They think it's haunted or something and say that thing on the top looks like a witch's hat!"

My dismay at his remark must have shown in my expression because he quickly apologized. "I'm sorry! I shouldn't have said that. After all, that's your home and I've upset you."

"It's *not* my *home!* I only am living there *temporarily* until my father —" I broke off. I wasn't really sure when my widowed father would send for me. It was something I longed for and kept hoping would happen. "And I'm *not upset!*" I declared indignantly. Suddenly my secret yearning for a *real* home with my *real* parent brought a rush of tears. I turned away so Jordan wouldn't see them.

But he had, and he put his hand on my chin and gently lifted my face, saying gently, "Hey, Julie, I *am* sorry. It was a stupid thing for me to say. I didn't mean to hurt your feelings. I think I understand. Both my parents are dead and Uncle Hugh's my guardian. He's putting me through school, but I miss having a real home, too."

Then he dug in his jacket pocket and brought out a clean handkerchief and dabbed my eyes. I think it may have been at that exact moment that I fell in love with him.

"Look, will you go skating again with me tomorrow night? It's going to be special. They're going to build bonfires around the pond, and the town band is going to provide music to skate by. Will you?"

Wanting so much to say yes, but knowing I'd have to get my aunt's permission first, I said doubtfully, "I'll have to ask Aunt Octavia —"

"Tell you what, I'll come by here at

seven," Jordan suggested. "And if it's all right for you to come, I'll be here waiting."

As it turned out, when I got into the house, I discovered Aunt Octavia had taken to her bed with *la grippe*. The next day Elvira came down with it, too, and I was able to slip out of the house to meet Jordan, no questions asked, no explanations necessary.

That whole evening came back to me as if it had happened yesterday: the clear, crystal air, sky hung with stars, my hand snug in Jordan's mittened one as we skated together to the strains of lilting melodies. That night he kissed me for the first time, his firm lips warm in the cold night.

We had the remaining days of the Christmas vacation to enjoy together. There was an excitement about our romance: maybe its secrecy intensified it. Because of their illness, neither Aunt Octavia nor Elvira knew that I was seeing Jordan. Only Toby was in on it. Sometimes he delivered my notes to Jordan or hid them in the hollow of an old tree we both knew about in the nearby woods. I kept all the ones Jordan left there for me, tucking them away under my pillow to read over and over.

Then the idyll ended. Holidays over, I had to go back to Merrivale, Jordan to medical school. But there was the summer to look

61

forward to, we told each other.

That summer was a magical time. Although Jordan had a job at the Woodvale hospital, we saw each other as much as possible. In September, when he saw me off on the train back to college, we knew we were in love. How could it all have ended so miserably in misunderstanding and heartbreak?

After I got back to Merrivale, I never heard from Jordan again. Suddenly there was silence. No answers to my desperate letters pleading for explanation. Nothing. Month after month I waited, sinking deeper and deeper into hopelessness. Didn't he mean the things he'd said? He'd told me that he loved me, that there could never be anyone else, that as soon as he finished medical school we would — How could he have forgotten? What of all our kisses, our passionate promises?

I didn't go back to Octagon House or to Woodvale the following summer. My father wrote that he wanted me to come and live with him, and I was glad to go, to forget Woodvale and how my heart had been broken.

I had never seen Jordan again — until today.

I buried my face in both my hands. I should never have come back here. I bitterly regretted my impulsive decision to return to Octagon House. It had always brought me unhappiness, and it would again.

Wearily I got undressed and into bed. Still I could not find relief in sleep, but lay staring into the darkness. Outside the moaning wind dragged the tree branches hoarsely across the windowpanes; inside the old house seemed full of strange noises and creaking sounds. Distantly I heard a clock strike one, then two. Restlessly I turned over, determinedly closed my eyes. Finally I drifted off.

Suddenly I was awake. Startled, I sat up in bed, clutching the covers, heart pounding. Something had awakened me, but I did not know what. Every nerve alert, every muscle tense, I strained, listening. What was it? The murmur of voices? Footsteps? Stealthy movement somewhere in the house — something.

I got up and padded across the floor in my bare feet. Quietly I inched open my bed-room door and peered out into the hall, into darkness. Cautiously I ventured out, then down the hall to the stairway. I saw a wavering light flickering from the stairwell. Moving slowly, I reached the banister and leaned over.

Outlined by the light from the candles

they held, two figures stood on the second-floor landing, their silhouettes casting grotesque shadows on the wall. Then I realized who they were. It was Miss Ingersoll, bundled in a bulky robe, her hair in a braid down her back, and Marshall.

What was Marshall doing in the house at this hour? Ever since I could remember, he had shared the apartment over the carriage house with the coachman.

I drew back, afraid they might be alerted by something and look up and see me. What on earth were they doing having a whispered conversation in the middle of the night? Suddenly I felt an irrational sort of fear. I turned and ran back to my room, my feet noiseless on the carpeted hallway.

I was shaking as I silently closed my door and leaned against it, breathless. There was something strange about what I had witnessed. Something even vaguely sinister.

Chapter Six

When I finally fell into a restless sleep, I woke up frequently, wondering about the scene I'd witnessed between Marshall and Miss Ingersoll. But then, nothing at Octagon House was simple or easily explained. It had always been like that, so why should I expect it to be any different now?

Some time near dawn I was awakened by a strange dream. One I could not even remember once I was fully awake. The room was filled with a murky grayness, and I got up to get myself a drink of water. Crossing the room, I stopped at the window for some reason, and as I stood there saw a figure moving toward the carriage barn. Who could it be at this hour? Marshall? Someone else? A tramp from the dense wood surrounding Octagon House? As I watched, the figure disappeared and I shuddered involuntarily.

I drank my water and went back to bed. But sleep did not easily come again. Too many questions — about my aunt, her reasons for inviting us back, about my cousins — demanded answers. Scenes from my childhood here flashed through my mind, vague incidents, voices, events, all confusing and troubling.

I don't know when I drifted off to sleep, but when I woke up the second time I was dull-headed and sandy-eyed and desperately in need of a cup of coffee. I got dressed and went down to the kitchen.

"You're up bright and early, Miss Julie," Lutie greeted me cheerfully.

"Early but not so bright," I quipped. "I didn't sleep too well."

Lutie gave me a quick glance. "Strange house, strange bed — I suppose . . ."

"It shouldn't be strange," I said. "After all, it was the room and bed I slept in for — how many years? Since I was almost ten. I'm nearly twenty-four, Lutie." I helped myself to coffee from the pot on the stove and sat down at the table. "I guess no one else is up yet?"

"No, but that shouldn't surprise you. Elvira was always a slug-abed, and remember how Toby had to be dragged out of bed? On school days, anyway! Leopards don't change their spots, and neither do people change their ways," Lutie said with a shake of her head.

66

"When I woke up earlier I thought I saw someone out on the lawn," I began.

Lutie's hands, sprinkling cinnamon and sugar on top of the turnovers, paused. "How early?"

"Very early. It was just getting light. I went back to bed."

Lutie went on sprinkling. "Well, it couldn't have been me. I only got here a few minutes before you came down," she said.

"Just got here? You mean —"

"I live in town now, Miss Julie. With my sister. There aren't any live-in servants at Octagon House anymore."

"No? Then who does the housework — the cleaning?" There used to be two maids all the time I lived here. Annie, who took care of the downstairs rooms, waxing, polishing, and helping with the serving, and Tessa, the upstairs maid, who was great fun and our ally against the grown-ups.

"There's day help comes in three times a week now. With only Miss Octavia and Mr. Victor, there really isn't that much to do. Besides, some of the rooms have been closed up for years. . . ." Lutie said.

I stirred sugar into my coffee. "And Marshall, where does —" I started to ask, but just then Miss Ingersoll bustled into the kitchen. On seeing me she stopped abruptly.

"Oh, I see you're up, Miss Madison," she said. "Well, you can relay this information to your cousins when they get up. Miss Octavia had a bad night and is going to stay in bed and rest today. Too much excitement, I'm sure, just as I predicted. I was up half the night with her."

"I hope it's not serious," I said. That must explain the midnight meeting between her and Marshall that I witnessed. Perhaps they had been discussing whether to send for Jordan.

Miss Ingersoll's face was as sour as a lemon as she replied, "I warned Miss Octavia that her condition would be aggravated with all the confusion of having people in the house. That she isn't up to this sort of thing. But she wouldn't listen. Insisted on having you three come." Miss Ingersoll's tone was martyred. Then she dismissed me with a look and turned to Lutie. "I'll take Miss Vale's tray up to her, Lutie, if it's ready."

"It is. The water's boiling for her tea now. I'll just pour it." Lutie gestured toward the white wicker bed tray on the counter. Miss Ingersoll turned and started rearranging things on the tray while Lutie filled a china teapot, slipped a quilted cozy over it, and placed it on the tray.

68

"I hope you'll inform your cousins that I don't want Miss Octavia disturbed today," Miss Ingersoll continued to me sternly. "She says she's coming down for dinner because of an important discussion she wants to have with you three, but we'll see if she's up to that later." Miss Ingersoll picked up the tray and started out of the kitchen.

"Yes, I will, Miss Ingersoll," I reassured her. "Don't worry about me. I'm going to take a walk down into Woodvale, see how it's changed."

The nurse halted at the door. "Oh, then, you'll be passing the library, won't you? Would you return some books for me? It will save me a trip. I'll put them on the hall table, and you can pick them up as you go out the door. I don't want to leave because Dr. Barret is coming to see Miss Octavia."

Hearing this, I hastily finished my coffee and got up. I wanted to be out of the house before Jordan came. The last thing in the world I wanted was the chance of running into him again.

Ten minutes later I stepped out on the veranda and started down the steps. Heavy clouds hovering overhead threatened rain, and halfway down the drive I debated as to whether I should go back and hunt for an umbrella to take along. But afraid that any delay

69

might heighten the risk of seeing Jordan, I decided to chance it and hurried on. As I opened the gate, then turned to shut it, I happened to look up at the house and saw a curtain move at one of the second-floor windows. As I looked, the curtain dropped, and I saw the shadow of a figure step back from the window. Someone was watching me!

How annoying, I thought, irritated. But I soon dismissed the incident as I walked on, interested in noting that little *had* changed in Woodvale. Walking along following the route I had always taken, I suddenly realized I was nearing the Barret house. I saw the sign on the post in front: DR. JORDAN BARRET, OFFICE HOURS, DAILY 3–5 P.M. Ducking my head, I scurried past, hoping Jordan was not at home to see me go by.

I went to the library first to return Miss Ingersoll's books. Pushing inside the door, I sniffed the nostalgic smells of books, paste, and ink pads. Behind the desk a small, gray-haired woman glanced up from the stack of books she was stamping, and looked at me curiously over her glasses.

"Yes? May I help you?" she asked.

"Just returning some books," I told her. "From Miss Ingersoll, Miss Vale's nurse at Octagon House. I'm Julie Madison, Miss Vale's niece. I'm just here visiting."

She gave a little nervous start, an anxious frown puckering her brow. "Oh, yes, of course. You're returning these for Miss Ingersoll? Not Mr. Vale?" She looked worried. "Does that mean Victor — I mean, Mr. Vale — won't be in today?" A slow flush moved over her face. "The reason I'm asking is that I've been helping, well, not really helping — just making some research available —" The more she said, the more flustered she became.

Feeling sorry for her, I tried to set her at ease by saying, "You must be Miss MacAndrews. Uncle Victor told us you've been so helpful to him."

She seemed embarrassed but pleased. "Well, I hope so. I'm very interested in the work Mr. Vale's doing. We share a common interest in Woodvale history."

"Well, I'm glad to meet you, Miss MacAndrews. I'll tell Uncle Victor and Aunt Octavia you were asking —"

"Oh, no, please don't do that!" Her face blanched. "I mean, I'll probably see him later — I mean, Mr. Vale usually stops in the library every day." Then she added quickly, "To check on his research!"

"Yes, of course," I said reassuringly. "Well, I have to be going now. Good-bye."

Poor thing! And poor Uncle Victor, I

71

thought as I left. Obviously neither he nor Miss MacAndrews wanted Aunt Octavia to know of their — what? Romantic relationship?

Uncle Victor was a distinguished-looking man, tall with erect bearing, immaculate grooming, silver hair and courtly manners. Why shouldn't he and the dowdy Miss MacAndrews find each other congenial companions? But why, at his age, should his sister so intimidate him? Did Aunt Octavia hold the purse strings? Was he afraid of her? Is that why Miss MacAndrews nearly panicked at the suggestion I might mention something to Aunt Octavia about Uncle Victor's daily visits to the library?

Well, Octagon House had always been a place of secrets. Mystery had always seemed to surround the Vale family. There were so many things about my own mother and her two brothers, Mark and Roger, Toby's and Elvira's fathers, I didn't know. How many other secrets were hidden at Octagon House?

Deep in thought I walked out of the library and onto the steps, and to my dismay, I saw it was raining.

"May I offer you a ride?" asked a hauntingly familiar voice.

Instinctively I tensed as Jordan Barret stepped out from behind the pillars and came toward me.

Chapter Seven

"My buggy is at the curb. I'm on my way to the hospital to make rounds, and I pass right by Octagon House."

I felt trapped. This was the very thing I'd rushed away from the house to avoid! As I hesitated, the heavens seemed to open up, and rain poured down relentlessly. It seemed ridiculous to refuse.

Jordan lifted an eyebrow, raised his large umbrella, and offered his arm. "Unless you'd rather go back inside the library and talk? I'm determined that we should talk."

He certainly looked determined. The alternative to being drenched was to endure this forced conversation. Still I hesitated. What was there possibly to say to each other after six years of silence?

"Don't be stubborn, Julie," he said at last.

Finally I said reluctantly, "Well, if you're sure this is what you want . . ."

A trace of a smile touched Jordan's lips. "Yes, Julie, it *is* what I want," he said firmly.

73

Then he placed his hand under my elbow, and we went down the library steps under his sheltering umbrella. He handed me carefully into the buggy, tucked my skirt in neatly before closing the low door, then went around the other side and climbed in beside me.

I stared straight ahead, not trusting myself to look at him, too aware of his nearness. Jordan was so close that I could smell the damp tweed of his coat, the faint antiseptic odor of his profession mixed with some kind of herbal scent. My heart thudded noisily as the rain pounded on the leather roof of the buggy.

I felt so uncomfortable I wondered if it might not have been better to make a dash for it instead of accepting Jordan's offer. It would have only meant soaked clothing, wet boots, and dripping hair. This was far more risky.

I wished myself anywhere else. The awkward silence between us stretched agonizingly. Why didn't Jordan pick up the reins and get going? I turned to see and found him regarding me gravely as if he had been waiting for me to look at him. Disconcerted, I blurted out an inane remark. "It's really coming down, isn't it? It was certainly lucky for me you came along when you did."

"Actually, luck had nothing to do with it, Julie. I saw you from my office window when you passed by, and I followed you. Ever since yesterday I knew I *had* to try to see you. I owe you an apology —"

"You don't owe me anything, Jordan," I protested uneasily.

"Yes, I do. I was inexcusably rude to you yesterday. My only excuse is that — it was a shock to see you again. And I didn't handle it well. I'm sorry about that."

I couldn't think of anything else to say but "It was a shock to see you too. I didn't know you'd come back to Woodvale or taken over your uncle's practice."

"I always planned to. Don't you remember?" he asked in a low voice.

I closed my eyes for a moment. I didn't want to remember those plans, those promises. They had all happened in another lifetime. Why was he bringing them up now? Ignoring his question, I blundered on, "And now you are my aunt's physician. She's certainly aged, so badly crippled . . ." I murmured.

"Crippled?" he repeated the word, frowning. "Yes, unfortunately, crippled emotionally as well as physically. Or maybe I should say more so. For her age your aunt could still be an active, healthy woman. Her mind is as bright and alert as ever. But she is so full of old resentments, old hatreds, that her body has absorbed them, reacting by becoming painfully twisted and increasingly immobile. Her blood pressure is dangerously high. She didn't tell me about her plans for this reunion. She knew I'd argue against it. Excitement is very bad for her. I have seen her become so enraged I feared she might have a stroke there and then."

"Enraged?" I echoed. "About what?"

"What's to become of Octagon House. That's her obsession," Jordan said flatly. "That is what keeps her in a constant state of turmoil. Anxiety, her regrets about the past, the people she has quarreled with, events she cannot change. It is all making her body sick."

Fascinated by such an idea, I listened with interest as he continued.

"There's been quite alot of interest in the effect of the emotions on a person's physical condition. Especially in Europe. Doctors there have made great strides in diagnosing these kinds of ailments. A sick body indicates a sick soul. The word *psyche* is the Greek word for 'soul.' The ancient Greek physicians saw this connection clearly, but doctors today are taking longer to accept it —"

"And what does my aunt think of your newfangled notions?" I could not resist asking, with some amusement, imagining myself what Aunt Octavia's reaction might have been.

Jordan shrugged. "Dismisses it as nonsense, of course. I haven't pursued it too vigorously. She just wants me to give her something to deaden the pain."

"That's understandable. She seems to have quite a lot of it."

"Everyone wants their pain deadened," Jordan said solemnly. "I certainly do. Don't you, Julie? Or did you get over us without too much pain? Did you find an antidote quickly, something — or *someone* — that made it easy?"

I faced him indignantly. "I don't know what you're talking about!"

"Don't you? Then why were all my letters returned from Merrivale stamped Refused?" he demanded.

"Refused? What do you mean?"

Jordan looked angry, then puzzled. "Just what I said. I tried writing again and again, and the letters always came back unopened, stamped Refused. I didn't know what had happened; I was bewildered, then very angry. When I came home that summer, I went straight to Octagon House and found you hadn't come back from college. I was told you had gone to live with your father, and Miss Vale told me she had no idea where he had taken you or how to get in touch with you, that you wanted to sever all your ties with Woodvale. I guessed that meant me, too. I was badly hurt — and terribly angry. That was a cruel thing to do, Julie."

I gazed at him speechlessly. "Jordan, I know nothing about all this!" I finally managed to exclaim. "I never got *any* letters from you after that summer. I wrote and wrote, but you never answered. I don't understand —"

"You mean — ?"

"Yes, of course. I *never* received a single letter after I got back to college. I couldn't imagine what had happened, except" — I stumbled over the words — "except I finally had to come to the conclusion that you weren't in love with me anymore. What else could I think?"

We stared at each other incredulously.

"What — where could those letters — what possibly could have happened?" Jordan said.

"The only possible explanation is someone intercepted them . . . somehow. . . . All our mail at Merrivale came through the main office and was distributed from there. They put our letters out on the table in the front hall of our dormitory. Each day when we came in from morning classes, that was the first thing all the girls checked. Mail was so important! Letters meant so much. I waited and waited for yours —" I shook my head in disbelief. "Did you *really* write?"

"Believe me, Julie, I did," Jordan said. "Did *you?*"

I nodded. "Yes, Jordan, I did."

"Then, how — ?"

"I don't know."

We sat there locked in a kind of stunned silence. Turbulent thoughts tumbled in confusion through my mind. All those years, all those miserable months I wept and waited to hear from Jordan, and now to find that all the hurt had been unnecessary. Someone had played with our lives. But who — and why?

Aunt Octavia's name came to my mind, but I rejected it. She didn't even know about Jordan and me. We'd kept our romance our secret, too precious to share with anyone. We'd been so careful, so clever — at least, we thought so.

The rain beat steadily outside as we continued to sit there in silence. Then Jordan reached over and took my cold hand, warming it in both of his, and asked softly, "Is it possible, do you think, to begin again?"

I turned and looked deep into those clear gray-blue eyes, seeing in them the same hope that stirred in my heart, the promise of something that I longed for and had thought forever lost.

"I don't know, Jordan. A lot of time has gone by, we've both changed —"

"We can try, can't we? Give ourselves a second chance?"

"I need time to think, Jordan. We both need to sort all this out. If somehow Aunt Octavia is responsible, in some way we can't figure out now — well, she's old and ill — I don't want to hate her."

"No! Hate is destructive. Pity is more what I feel for her — whatever she's done." He picked up the reins then, slapped them, and the horse started forward. We rode silently along the streets, up the hill, turned in the drive, and stopped finally under the porte cochere.

Seen through a veil of rain Octagon House looked gloomier and more forbidding than ever. Jordan looked up at it and said fiercely, "That house! I still don't like going in there. It has a malevolent atmosphere you notice even before you step inside. Maybe, because there's been so much unhappiness, so much conflict —" He stopped, looking contrite. "Sorry, I guess my old antagonism to it and people like your aunt is surfacing."

"I understand. I feel the same way. I didn't really want to come back, but something drew me. . . ."

Jordan looked at me, his eyes tender, and he said quietly, "Don't be sorry you came, Julie. Maybe it was meant to be. Maybe it was Fate trying to right old wrongs."

I smiled. "What a thing for a man of science to say. You sound like Lutie. Now, *she* really believes in *Fate*."

"We must see each other again, Julie. There is so much to talk about, so much I want to tell you, so much I want to know about all the years in between."

"Yes, I know."

"I'll check my schedule — work out some free time. I'll send a note, then we'll make plans. It's difficult, you know; I'm the only doctor in town."

"I understand."

I looked up at the house and involuntarily shuddered. Mistaking it for a shiver, Jordan said solicitously, "You're cold; we've been sitting out in all this dampness too long. You better go inside."

But I didn't want to go inside. What Jordan had said about Octagon House was true. Unhappiness and conflict had always been there. Each of our parents — Toby's, Elvira's and mine — had left it in the midst of turmoil, never to return. There was something terrible there that compelled people to escape. But there was nothing else to do, no other place for me to go.

Jordan got out, came around, and helped me step down. "I'll see you soon, Julie," he said, and there was an eagerness in his voice.

"Perhaps we best not say anything to the others," I suggested haltingly, "especially Aunt Octavia."

Jordan's brows came together in a straight line above furious eyes. "You mean keep our meeting secret? No, Julie, there have been too many secrets at Octagon House, too much hidden. Besides, *she* has no control over us anymore."

I made no comment, but as I watched his buggy disappear around the curve of the drive, I thought, He's wrong, Aunt Octavia still controls everything and everyone at Octagon House. That's why she is so dangerous.

Chapter Eight

As I started to close the front door behind me, a strong gust of wind caught it, wresting it from my hand. It slammed shut, rattling the etched-glass panels. Thrust forward myself by the strength of the draft, I nearly collided with Miss Ingersoll.

She looked taken aback by my sudden stumbling entrance and our near impact. Her gooseberry eyes widened in surprise.

I was just as startled, and as I tried to regain my balance, I saw a look of resentment or dislike cross her face before a forced smile stretched her lips.

"Miss Madison!" she exclaimed. "Nasty weather! But rain or shine, out I go for my daily constitutional." She tightened the scarf around her head and bustled past me out the door and down the steps.

I had the distinct feeling that she must have been standing right inside the front door watching Jordan and me through the glass panels. Spying on us? For what purpose? I wondered what conclusion she had drawn from observing us. What a strange person our aunt's nurse was, I thought as I took off my hat and hung my coat up on the coat tree.

She had been at Octagon House so long she seemed to feel she owned it and that we three cousins were intruders. Maybe she just resented us coming and upsetting the established routine. She had certainly made that clear enough

"Well, where have you been all morning?" Elvira's voice, sounding injured, demanded, and I turned to see her at the door of the small parlor. "It's been dull as can be around here. I came down this morning and found you gone, and Toby disappeared somewhere without telling anyone. Aunt Octavia's been resting all day and left word she was not to be disturbed! I've been playing Patience by myself for hours. I'm about at my wit's end. Do come in and keep me company, for pity's sake!"

I would rather have gone up to my room and been alone to think my own thoughts, to ponder all the things Jordan and I had discussed. But I didn't want to arouse Elvira's curiosity by acting secretive. I thanked my lucky stars that the parlor room windows did not face the driveway, so she could not have seen Jordan bring me back from town. I wasn't up to one of Elvira's inquisitions.

Anyway, I could tell she had something on her mind. Something she could not wait to talk about. She looked down the hall both ways before closing the door carefully, then turned to me, saying in a conspiratorial voice, "We have to talk about why Aunt Octavia asked us all here."

I did not react immediately, feeling sure Elvira would tell me her opinion.

She looked annoyed and flung herself on the sofa, crossed her legs, and impatiently swung one narrow foot in its bronze leather, high-heeled French boot. "Oh, you're as irritating as Toby!" she accused. "You're both so — so —"

"What? What are we, Elvira?" Toby asked as his tousled red head poked through the door. "Is this a private meeting, or can anyone attend?"

"Idiot!" Elvira said. "Come on in, but shut the door. I have a feeling even the walls have ears in this place! I was just telling Julie we need to figure out why we were asked to come back to Octagon House."

"I think it's just one of Aunt Octavia's devious ways of torturing us," Toby said. "Reminds me of how she used to delay telling us what our punishment was going to be. Don't you remember? When we did something against the rules or got caught in some scrape, we'd first get a severe reprimand. Then she'd tell us she would have to think what kind of punishment fit our particular crime, and she'd keep us waiting forever before telling us what it was going to be. What a tyrant!" He grimaced. "Anyone join me in a sherry?"

"It's a little early, isn't it?" Elvira said acidly, giving Toby a disapproving look.

"Speak for yourself, Elvira," Toby said nonchalantly and helped himself to a glass from the decanter on the side table.

Elvira ignored him and returned to her point. "I want to know what you two think before I tell you what I believe is behind all this. So what's your opinion, Toby?"

"About what?" Toby's reply was as indolent and unconcerned as Elvira's question was sharp and peevish.

I suppressed a smile; I knew Toby was being purposely obtuse just to vex Elvira.

"For heaven's sake, Toby, what do you think I mean? *The* question — why were we all summoned here?"

Toby swirled the ruby liquid in his glass, held it up to the light as if studying its clarity, then replied indifferently, "How should I know, Elvira? I could never figure Aunt Octavia's reasons for doing anything. I'm certainly not going to try now."

"Then why in heaven's name did you come?" Elvira snapped.

"Curiosity, maybe. A free train ticket, lodging, meals. Maybe just for 'Auld Lang Syne.'" Toby smiled his roguish smile and circled the room slowly before settling down in the wing chair that was unofficially Aunt Octavia's "throne," as we used to call it when we were children.

"Well, I could give you a good dozen possibilities," began Elvira, then added, "but I really can't see —" She broke off uncertainly. "It really is a mystery, not hearing a word from her all these years, then suddenly this urgent letter to come. It's really strange."

"Maybe we should ask Lutie. Couldn't she always predict the future?" Toby teased.

Elvira sat up straight, her green eyes widening with excitement. "What a brilliant idea, Toby. Let's!" She looked at me, then Toby, then back at me again. "Remember what fun that always was? Anyway, it will while away this long, boring afternoon. Come on, to the kitchen, you two. We'll get Lutie to tell our fortunes." She was on her feet, pulling me up and motioning Toby with her other hand. "Come on, Toby, it'll be a lark. And who knows, one of us may have a real fortune in our future," she added enigmatically, dragging me along with her to the door.

It took some coaxing and convincing to assure Lutie that three adults were serious about having her tell their fortunes. She had just set her loaves of bread out to rise when we came in, clamoring for her to accommodate our whim.

"Well, now, let me make a fresh pot of coffee, and then we'll see whatever there is to see," she finally consented.

Lutie was Danish and made coffee the "old country" way so that there were grounds in the bottom of the cup. We waited until the coffee cooled, then each drank our cup, careful not to disturb the grounds at the bottom so Lutie could examine the shapes that were left.

She took my cup first, swirled it, turned it upside down on the saucer, then quickly righted it. "That way you empty out all the tears!" she said and beamed just as she had when we were young and begged her to read our fortunes.

For some reason, on this rainy afternoon, I felt that old thrill of anticipation as Lutie peered into the grounds.

"Now, look here — good luck all the way. Two good signs. See these lines? They form an 'open road.' That means something very exciting is coming. A change. See this circle? My, yes, Miss Julie, I see pleasant things ahead. Now, there's an unusual thing — the circle and a crescent both in one cup."

Elvira, beside me, was leaning forward breathing fast. "Do mine next, Lutie," she urged.

Lutie took her cup and went through the little ritual. When she lifted the cup from the saucer, we were surprised to see that most of the grounds had spilled out.

"My goodness! That's only happened a couple of times when I've read cups!" Lutie exclaimed.

"What does it mean?" Elvira asked eagerly.

"It's very rare. . . ." Lutie spoke slowly. "It means the subject has just reached a great decision. A burden of some kind has been lifted by this decision. Now, I can read some of that the way the grounds formed on the saucer. You're surely a person who has a strong, active personality, craves excitement, movement, activity. And if the grounds don't lie, you will get your heart's desire."

Elvira sat back with a smug smile.

"How about Toby?" I asked.

"All right, let's have a look at Mr. Toby's cup." Lutie reached for his cup and went through the same routine. "Now, here's a fellow with a lot of courage," she declared. "There's good luck coming in the not too distant future. See how the grounds cling to the middle of the cup? See that tree shape at the bottom? This person looks forward to happiness from a long way off, as though it never was going to happen to him. But it is, Toby. Be patient, wait and see. It's coming for you."

"Oh, that was fun, Lutie, thank you," I said.

Lutie got up from her chair, saying, "Well, how about some more coffee and some of my apple cake?"

Before she turned to the stove, I saw the expression on Lutie's face. It sent a chill all through me. Something had disturbed Lutie. Had she read something foreboding in one of our cups?

The readings had been brief, to say the least, with none of the enhancement of the fortunes Lutie used to tell, nothing about "tall, dark, and handsome strangers" or "finding a buried treasure," none of those tantalizing predictions that had always made this experience so delightful.

When she brought the cake back to the

table, our eyes met for a single second, and my impression was confirmed. Lutie looked away quickly, and I knew that she realized I suspected something and did not want me getting any indication of what troubled her.

Elvira and I had always been convinced Lutie's readings *were* authentic, that she did have "second sight," "the gift," or whatever folklore called it. Although she *said* it was all nonsense, I was sure Lutie believed it, too.

Now I was positive that Lutie had seen something in one of our cups that she had not wanted to tell. Was it in mine? Or Toby's? Or Elvira's?

I glanced at my cousins. Toby was leaning relaxedly in his tipped-back chair while Elvira argued with him heatedly. He was baiting her good-naturedly.

"I think you actually believe all this hocus-pocus, don't you?"

"Well, if you weren't so ignorant, Toby, you'd realize that there is new evidence that proves it is not all 'hocus-pocus,' as you call it. Even Scotland Yard has brought in clairvoyants to help them solve some difficult cases by finding missing people or bodies! And in New York last year many prominent people I know were consulting a noted medium, Madame Zavana, and holding seances."

Toby hooted. Elvira got up with haughty dignity and said scathingly, "Obviously you are not *au courant,* Toby, or you would not scoff at the meeting of science and the metaphysical. . . ."

As Elvira launched into a long, complicated story about some Wall Street banker who had disappeared without a trace and whose family employed this Madame whatever her name was, my attention was caught by Lutie's uncharacteristic nervousness. She seemed to grow increasingly uncomfortable at the trend of Elvira's arguments.

Was Lutie actually one of those special gifted people who *could* see through the veil into the supernatural and predict the future? If so, what had she seen in one of our cups that had upset her so much?

Chapter Nine

We were all a little on edge when we gathered in the drawing room that evening. Dinner had been particularly strained, probably because we all knew that afterward Aunt Octavia was going to reveal the reason behind her unexpected invitation to us. Our aunt never did anything without motivation.

Prolonging the suspense, as Toby had reminded us earlier, was also typical of her. Watching her now as she lingered over her demitasse, I wondered if she had really been instrumental in breaking up the romance between Jordan and me, and if so, how she had accomplished it.

Was I the only one feeling the underlying stress in the room? I glanced around at everyone. Elvira was holding forth about a controversial new play by Oscar Wilde that she and her husband had seen on a recent trip to London. Toby was sulking. Before Aunt Octavia had come down to join us before dinner, he and Elvira had got into it, and I could see he was still seething.

I had been the first one downstairs and was already in the drawing room when Elvira appeared. She looked even more glamorous than she had the evening before, in a Spanish-style bolero jacket embroidered with gold threads worn over a gracefully flared skirt of some kind of shimmering material.

I was wearing my blue merino again, and she gave me a cool once-over but refrained from making any schoolmarm comments. She seemed preoccupied, and I guessed she was thinking about what kind of pronouncement Aunt Octavia was going to make. Then we heard the front door slam, and a minute later Toby walked in.

He had obviously been out in the rain, for his hair was wet, a few wayward curls plastered to his forehead. His cheeks were flushed, and as he moved toward the fireplace rubbing his chapped-looking hands together, I noticed his jacket was quite damp. Didn't Toby have an overcoat? If he did, why had he gone out in the downpour without it?

"I'd forgotten what a miserable climate Woodvale has!" he declared, shuddering. "I could use a hot toddy to warm me up." He glanced over to the tray with the wineglasses and decanter of sherry on it that Marshall had brought in earlier and looked disappointed. "I suppose there's nothing stronger than *that?*"

"Beggars can't be choosers!" Elvira quoted insinuatingly.

Toby shot her a look of mock astonishment. "Are you defining me as a *beggar?*"

"You always were one," Elvira said acidly. "No matter when we all got our allowance, you always owed yours to someone and had to borrow."

"Not from *you!*" Toby flung back at her. "I'd get it from Lutie or borrow it from Julie. *You* were always too damn stingy, Elvira."

"Not *stingy,* Toby, just careful. And much too smart to lend you money. Did you ever pay Lutie or Julie back? I imagine not," she said archly, then added, "And I'd watch your language, Toby!"

"This sounds like the old days," a voice from the doorway said. "You two squabbling."

We turned to see Aunt Octavia. I wondered how long she had been there and if she had overheard what had been said.

Elvira at once became the epitome of graciousness. "Good evening, Aunt Octavia. How well you look this evening; your rest must have done you good." She was at our aunt's side immediately, placing a hand on her arm to lead her to her chair. "Would you like to be a little closer to the fire? It's so chilly tonight. Toby, help me pull her chair forward some. Julie, hand me that pillow for Aunt Octavia's back." Elvira issued us orders like a drill sergeant. Toby threw me a knowing glance.

"Stop fussing, Elvira, you're as bad as Ingersoll," Aunt Octavia said crossly.

That's the way the evening had begun, and dinner was even worse. Uncle Victor was not there, and no explanation was given for his absence. Conversation lagged painfully; no subject was brought up that sparked much response or resulted in any stimulating discussion. Everyone was relieved when dinner ended.

Now we all sat, mentally holding our breath, the tension tangible.

Finally Aunt Octavia put down her coffee cup, settled back in her chair, and surveyed us all. "Well, now I'll get to the point. I wanted you all here because what I have to say concerns you all. It concerns Victor, too, and he would have been here if it had been possible for me to discuss this last night. But tonight is the meeting of the Woodvale Historical Society, and since he is its secretary, he had to be there instead."

Her shiny black eyes darted back and forth, resting on one after the other of us for a single second, and then she began to speak, slowly and deliberately. "My father, Clement Vale, died and left the entire Vale estate to his wife, my stepmother, *your* Grandmother Vale. In his will he stipulated that at *her* death the estate should be inherited jointly by the children of his first marriage, that is Victor and me, and *your* parents, the children of his second marriage. I, as the oldest child of the two families, was appointed executrix of both my father's and stepmother's will, given power of attorney for the estate with the authority to manage it until my half brothers and half sister reached their majority. Unfortunately, each of the other Vale children died *before* my stepmother, and no provision was made for any of their children if they married."

Elvira moved nervously; Toby sat up straighter; my hands tightened in my lap. I had no idea what was coming next.

"Obviously, I am getting older and am not in good health. Victor is only two years younger and has never had a head for business or management." Aunt Octavia paused significantly. Looking around at the three of us, she continued, "The time has come when I must make some important decisions regarding the future of the Vale property. In the last few years, as our supply of timber has decreased, the mill has not been operating at full capacity on any of the three shifts. These conditions have naturally made inroads into the principal of the estate. Property taxes alone take an enormous amount of money. Maintaining this house and grounds is expensive, although, as you must have noticed, I have reduced the household staff and no longer keep several carriages or a stable of fine horses as we used to." Aunt Octavia paused dramatically before saying, "So, I have come to the conclusion that a new will should be drawn up in which *one* of *you three* will be designated as sole heir."

I heard Elvira's quick intake of breath. Toby was suddenly motionless. I was dumbfounded.

"It seemed only reasonable that one person should be given full responsibility. With the way your three lives have gone thus far — each of you living in a different part of the country, out of touch with me and one another — no joint control would be possible. You are all still young, all under thirty. So there is time for whomever I decide should become the sole inheritor to prepare, to train, to learn the management, the responsibilities necessary to be in charge of the vast holdings of this large estate. We are talking about a fortune in property, stocks, bonds, and investments of various kinds, to say nothing of this valuable house, its furnishings, artifacts, paintings, antiques, etcetera."

A disquieting silence fell. The sighing of the fire was the only sound until Aunt Octavia began speaking again.

"Perhaps this seems unfair. Perhaps you feel the estate should be cut up and divided now among the heirs. But after much thought and consultation with my lawyers, I believe this is the best way to handle the estate my father entrusted to me. The next question in your minds, I'm sure, is which one of you will be chosen for this great responsibility."

She stopped, and again, one by one, she glanced around the room, her eyes pausing on each of us in turn. At last she said, "*That* has not yet been decided. I have not yet made my choice. That is why you are here. I wanted to see for myself what kind of adults the children I'd reared here at Octagon House had become — who was worthy of this heavy responsibility, this great task. I will use this time to talk at length with each of you, find out what your abilities are, how you measure up to the job. I have no favorite, no predecided choice. It will remain to be seen who, in the end, will be chosen."

Suddenly Miss Ingersoll came into the room. I could not help but wonder if she had been outside in the hall, eavesdropping on this family meeting. Ignoring us, she went right over to Aunt Octavia.

"Excuse me, Miss Octavia, but it is time for your medication. Remember, Dr. Barret said to be *sure* to take it every four hours. It's nearly nine-thirty and —"

As if on cue, the mantel clock began to strike.

"Oh, all right, Ingersoll!" Aunt Octavia scowled and struggled to her feet, avoiding Miss Ingersoll's attempt to help her. To us, she said, "Well, anyway, I've said everything I have to say for tonight. In the next few days I will have the opportunity of talking to each of you individually, finding out what you've done, what experience you've had, what skills you've acquired since leaving Octagon House, and what your plans for the future are." Aunt Octavia was standing now, and she accepted Miss Ingersoll's arm and started toward the door. "Good night to you all," she called over her shoulder.

In unison we echoed, "Good night, Aunt Octavia," then looked at each other, embarrassed, feeling like a children's chorus.

As soon as Aunt Octavia was out of hearing distance, Elvira went over to close the drawing room door. Then she whirled around, giving her train a little kick, and glaring at us, hissed, "That wretched woman! Isn't it just like her to pit us all against one another like this?"

Toby strolled over to the piano, lifted the lid, sat down, and ran his fingers along the keys.

"Oh, stop it, Toby. It sounds off-key. It must need tuning," Elvira said angrily, wringing her thin hands.

Toby ignored her and began to play softly as he quoted in measured tones the old sing-song about the wheel of fortune. "Round and round she goes, and where she stops, nobody knows." Then he chuckled. "When Aunt Octavia finds out how I've spent the years since I left Octagon House, I won't have a chance." He looked at me. "You may be the lucky one, Julie."

I started to protest, Not *me!* I don't want it! but I didn't have a chance because Elvira rushed in furiously.

"*I'm* the oldest! I should be chosen. I've handled Drew's and my finances ever since we got married or nearly —" She stopped midsentence, realizing that was *not* exactly

101

how she had presented her husband to us before. She had told us he was a stock-broker, an investment counselor to wealthy clients.

"And *I'm* the only *male,* the only one who carries the *Vale* name," Toby said.

"Don't forget *Uncle Victor,*" Elvira reminded him sharply.

"Aunt Octavia's already ruled him out, remember?" Toby retorted.

I felt sickened by this discussion. The last thing I wanted, fortune or no fortune, was to be trapped at Octagon House for the rest of my life trying to manage an estate! I wished I'd never come. I wished I could leave right now. If there were a midnight train, I would! Then I thought of Jordan and the possibility of our renewed romance, and my wild impulse to leave subsided.

However, I did not want to be part of the ugly guessing game Toby and Elvira were indulging in, so I got up and walked to the door. "I've got a headache," I told them. "I'm going to bed."

They both looked at me skeptically. But not caring whether they believed me or not, I left. I needed to be alone. As I walked upstairs and along the dimly lit halls to my bedroom, I felt the strong aversion I'd felt earlier that afternoon upon reentering the house after being with Jordan.

He was right, I thought, this house holds a strange residue from a family torn by strife, within these walls lingers the echoes of all the angry scenes, the unforgiving words, the violent emotions that have raged here in the past. And now, I was very afraid, more tragedy was going to take place at Octagon House.

Chapter Ten

Once alone in my bedroom I allowed my own feelings about Aunt Octavia's plan to surface. It seemed particularly manipulative. In spite of the years of separation, we three still cared about one another. But with this inheritance plan, she was making us rivals for a fortune that should, by rights, be divided equally among the heirs.

But then, I asked myself, why should I be shocked or appalled? What Aunt Octavia had done was entirely in keeping with her character and how she had always dealt with us.

When we were children here, she had tried the same kind of tactics, playing favorites, trying to get us to tattle on one another to escape some threatened punishment, withholding permission to one, granting it to another. Somehow we had managed to stick together, remain friends, hold out against her manipulation. Over the years we may have lost touch, but I didn't think we had changed so much that we would now turn against one another.

A peremptory rap on the door broke into my thoughts, followed by Elvira's voice on the other side, demanding, "Julie! You're not asleep yet, are you? Let me in, I have to talk to you!"

Reluctantly I went to the door and opened it. "Elvira, I'm very tired, and I told you I have a headache —"

"What of it? So do I!" she retorted. "Who wouldn't have a headache after tonight?" Brushing past me into the room, Elvira kept right on talking. "That dreadful woman! It's despicable what she's doing. We should all have an equal share. We all have as much right as she has to inherit part of this estate." She started pacing back and forth. "It must be worth hundreds of thousands of dollars! Can you just imagine what that could mean to *me?* I mean *us* — all of us. I *know* Toby needs money." She stopped prowling around the room and whirled around, shaking her forefinger at me. "And don't tell me you couldn't use a nice little inheritance, Julie! Surely your father didn't leave you a fortune. Not from the salary of a college teacher!"

"But, Elvira, I hate what Aunt Octavia is doing as much as you do. I don't want any-

105

thing to do with any of this!"

Elvira stared at me, momentarily speechless at my statement. Then, never at a loss of words for long, she dismissed it curtly. "Don't be such a fool, Julie. You may think that now, but when you've had time to think this through, you'll change your mind. It's not as though you had a choice any more than Toby and I do. *Your* mother was as much a Vale as Aunt Octavia, and if for no other reason but loyalty to *her* you should be willing to fight for your share."

Elvira's face was pale, so pale that her freckles showed underneath the heavy layer of rice powder she applied to cover them. Her expression was grim, defensive. She paused, as if deep in thought, her hand on her chin, the large emerald sparkling on her finger. Then she spoke with determination.

"Now, listen to what I have to say, Julie. One of us is going to be named heir. It doesn't matter much *which* one — that is, if we all agree to what I have in mind." Her green eyes were flashing fire as she continued rapidly, "We can all come out of this much wealthier than we ever dreamed and with no appreciable diminishing of the principal of the estate to whichever one of us inherits. No one will go home empty-handed. But the main thing is that *whoever* inherits must immediately apply for power of attorney to make the necessary decisions —"

"Elvira, I meant what I said," I cut in. "I don't even want to discuss this —"

"Oh, for heaven's sake, Julie, will you hear me out? You can't play the innocent. Or be an ostrich hiding your head in the sand. This is real life, Julie; we all have a stake in what happens here. We *have* to discuss it — the three of us —"

"Well, then, where is Toby?" I demanded, "How does he feel about what you're proposing?"

Elvira made a disgusted face. "Oh, there was no use talking to Toby tonight. He's downstairs getting quietly drunk. He'll be sick as a dog tomorrow with all that sweet sherry." She halted, frowning. "But, of course, I don't mean to leave Toby out in the cold, or *you*, and *I* certainly don't intend to be." Her face hardened.

I could feel my temples pounding and I said wearily, "Well, let's wait until tomorrow, Elvira. I don't think we should discuss this any more tonight. Not without Toby."

She opened her mouth slightly as if she were about to say something else, then closed it promptly, evidently deciding against it. She moved to the door; with her hand on the doorknob she turned back to me.

"Julie, keep this in mind. We always stuck together as children. That's how we survived Aunt Octavia's destructive influence on us when we were growing up here. We have to do that now." Her eyes held me compellingly so that I could not look away. I nodded and Elvira left.

If I had found it hard to go to sleep the first night I was back at Octagon House, the second night it was almost impossible. I tossed and turned, and when I managed to fall into a shallow sleep, I had nightmares. Wakening, I found every muscle taut, every nerve stretched, and myself sleepless again.

The house seemed full of mysterious sounds: scurrying, scraping, and scuffling. Muted footsteps on the carpeted hall outside my door? I was aware of movement overhead. Something being dragged or pushed? But the top floor was empty, unoccupied now that no servants stayed there and the attic was used only for storage. Was it just nerves and an overactive imagination? Every old house had all sorts of creaks and unidentifiable sounds, I told myself. But in the middle of the night they were more disturbing.

Restless, I got up and walked over to the

window and looked out. Rain battered against the window; a fierce wind rattled the glass in its frame and whipped the bare tree branches. I shivered and went back to bed and drew the covers around me. I lay there listening to the wind whistling around the corners of the house and howling high up in the cupola, until finally, exhausted, I fell asleep again.

The next time I woke it was dawn. I was wide awake and knew I could not go back to sleep nor get any more rest. I had too much on my mind. I got up and saw it had stopped raining. Fog dripped eerily from the low-hanging branches of the trees; in the gray light heavy clouds moved sluggishly over-head. Suddenly I felt the need to get out, away from this house. Maybe the cool, rain-washed air would clear the cobwebs from my confused mind and help me decide what I should do.

After dressing quickly, I went down the stairs and through the hall into the kitchen, carrying my boots so as not to make any sound. No one was there. There was no fire in the stove. It was too early for Lutie. I pulled on my boots, wrapped a long knitted scarf over my head and around my neck, then went out the back door.

Bending my head against the cold wind,

I headed across the drive, past the carriage house, and took the path leading into the woods. The density of the towering fir trees created a silence that was almost complete. Nothing stirred or moved, no chirping of awakening birds nor rustling of small woodland creatures. My footsteps were soundless on the wet, matted pine needles.

The mist rising from the ground cloaked everything, obscuring the path ahead. I seemed to step into it, and it would close behind me like some kind of mysterious veil. But these silent woods, unlike the house I had just fled, held no terror for me. This was a walk I'd taken often when I lived at Octagon House, especially when I was upset, angry at Aunt Octavia, or had quarreled with Elvira.

I was struggling with the same three conditions now.

These woods also reminded me of Jordan. They were our meeting place during that romantic summer. The thought of Jordan and the conclusion we had come to about someone tampering with our letters only added to my confusion. Could Aunt Octavia have found out about us and somehow been responsible?

But *why* would she have done it? Certainly Jordan was not in any way unsuitable.

His uncle, Dr. Hugh Barret, had been the family physician for years. Why would she have objected to his nephew? And if Aunt Octavia disliked Jordan, why would she now have him as her doctor?

Completely absorbed in my troubled thoughts, I walked on with no clear direction, one thought tumbling on the next. The more I tried to figure things out, the worse it got. Now there was this thing about the will and the inheritance.

Elvira had been livid last night. I knew Elvira, and when she was aroused, she was as tenacious as Aunt Octavia. Our aunt had put something treacherous in motion, and there was no knowing how it would end.

All at once I halted on the path. I wasn't sure why. The wind picked up suddenly, sweeping through the trees with a mournful, sighing sound. A twig snapped behind me and I jumped. I looked over my shoulder. Did a figure just duck behind a tree a few feet from me? My heart jolted and started throbbing. I could feel a prickling along my scalp. Was I being followed?

Tramps often camped out in these woods. Aunt Octavia used to warn us about coming out here alone when we were children. Panic rushed up in me.

I took one step forward, then another. I

quickened my pace, and then I began to run. Were booted feet gaining on me, or was it my own heart's pounding I heard? Wild with fright, I looked behind me, and as I did I tripped over a tree root and stumbled. I flung both hands out in front of me to break my fall as I fell flat on the ground.

Gasping for breath, I staggered to my feet. Convinced now there *was* someone getting closer, someone out to do me harm, I tried to run faster, but the dampened hem of my heavy wool skirt dragged, slowing me. I slipped and slid on the wet pine needles. Out of breath, my legs weakening, I had to stop, needed desperately to catch my breath. I reached out with one hand and leaned against the rough bark of a tree, then glanced back fearfully.

To my horror, I saw a tall figure advancing toward me through the fog. I tried to scream, but nothing came out; my fist was pressed against my mouth. As the dark shape came closer, I shrank back against the tree trunk, braced for an assault.

Then I heard a man's voice call, "Julie!" and Jordan appeared out of the enveloping mist.

Disbelief and then thankfulness washed over me. "Oh, Jordan! Jordan! It's *you!* Thank goodness!"

He came up to me. "What are you doing out here? What is it? What's wrong?"

Weak with relief I gasped, "I'm so glad to see you." I told him in a shaky voice, "I thought — I thought someone — but I guess it was you all the time. How did you happen to be in the woods?"

"I've been at the hospital most of the night with a patient. He's past the crisis, and I needed to get some fresh air. I just took this path — I don't know exactly why. But I'm glad I did." He looked down at me, his brow furrowed. "You look frightened half to death, Julie. What's going on?"

"So much. Oh, Jordan, it's awful. I wish I'd never come back here, back to Woodvale."

He put both hands on my shoulders, looked into my face, and said earnestly, "Don't say that, Julie. I was just thinking about you, about *us*. That it's the one good thing in my life right now, you coming back here just when you did."

"But, Jordan, if you only knew what was going on at Octagon House." I had to steel myself not to put my head on his shoulder and allow him to hold me, comfort me.

"I'll walk you back and you can tell me." He slipped my hand through his arm, and we turned and started back through the woods in the direction of Octagon House while I told him about Aunt Octavia's pronouncement. He listened attentively as I poured out the whole plan and Elvira's reaction.

"I haven't had a chance to talk to Toby yet. But I will later today. It's a dreadful, divisive thing she's done, and I don't know what's going to happen. I just wish I could leave."

We were at the edge of the woods by now. I could see lights on in the kitchen windows and smoke coming out of the chimney. Lutie must be there and busy about breakfast.

"Julie, I have to go back to the hospital now to check on my patient. This afternoon I'm scheduled to go over to Perrysville to see some patients too old and infirm to make it to my office. Why not drive over there with me? It would get you away from Octagon House for a few hours. It would give us a chance to talk, too. We owe that to ourselves, Julie. Please say yes."

"I'm not sure I can, Jordan —"

"Try, Julie," he urged. "If you can manage it, come over to my house by three. I should be home, but if I'm delayed at the hospital, my housekeeper, Mrs. Hammond, will be there."

I looked up into his eyes. Suddenly they seemed the only thing I could trust, the only thing that promised sanity in the madness that was going on at Octagon House.

"Yes, Jordan, I will try," I promised. "I must go in now. Or there'll be too much to explain."

I hurried across the stretch of yard to the back porch. At the kitchen door I turned and looked back; Jordan was still standing where I'd left him, watching me. I raised my hand and waved, then reluctantly opened the door and reentered Octagon House.

Chapter Eleven

Lutie turned around from the stove as I came inside. She took one look at me and exclaimed, "My land, Julie! You look like you seen a ghost! Whatever have you been doing out on such a morning as this?"

Stepping into the warmth of the kitchen from the damp, chill morning and after my scare, I suddenly realized how cold I was. I began to shiver.

"Here, you sit down right this minute." Lutie pulled out a chair at the table for me. "I'll pour you a good hot cup of coffee. That's what you need, and maybe a bowl of oatmeal. That'll warm you up."

I did as she suggested, and as soon as she placed the steaming mug in front of me, I clasped it with both hands, inhaling the fragrance as I brought it up to my lips.

Lutie stood, her hands on her ample hips, looking at me severely. "Whatever possessed you to go out on this kind of a morning? Fog as thick as pea soup."

116

The mug halfway to my mouth, I halted and stared at her. "Do you ever stay over, Lutie?" I asked, remembering some of the inexplicable noises I'd heard in the night. "I thought, maybe in bad weather, like last night, you might stay in your old room upstairs."

"Oh, my, no, Miss Julie. In bad weather my nephew comes for me."

That settled any simple explanation of the nocturnal disturbances. Then I thought of my scare in the woods. Did Lutie use the path on her way to work? Was it possible I'd mistaken Lutie for someone following me?

"How do you get here in the morning so early, Lutie? Surely you don't walk, do you? You don't come through the woods?"

Lutie looked surprised. "Through the woods, miss? Not on your life." I thought she gave a little shudder. "On mornings like this my nephew brings me. He works at the bakery and has to be in early. He lets me off right at the gate." She turned back to the stove and stirred the bubbling oatmeal.

I sipped my coffee thoughtfully. The more I thought about it, the more sure I was that someone had been following me in the woods. Jordan had said that he'd come from the hospital. The two paths crossed at a fork in the path close to Octagon House; one

117

path led to the road, the other circled and ended up behind the barn and carriage house. Maybe I had disturbed some tramp's make shift shelter as I came through, and he had followed me out of curiosity. Probably no one much went through those woods anymore.

"What about Marshall, Lutie? He still stays on the place, doesn't he?"

"Oh, yes, in the apartment over the carriage barn. He used to share it with Tim, the coachman; they were both bachelors then. But Tim got married and lives in town, so Marshall has the place to himself." She paused and placed a bowl of oatmeal down in front of me, slid the sugar bowl closer, and poured thick cream into a small pitcher and put it down alongside. "Now, you eat up, Miss Julie. You need your nourishment. You're way too thin, you and Elvira both, nothing but skin and bones."

I set down my coffee mug. "And what about Miss Ingersoll, does she sleep on the top floor?"

Lutie raised her eyebrows in alarm. "Who? Her? No, miss, she has her own rooms adjoining Miss Octavia's. No one uses the top floor anymore. Mrs. Henshaw retired and Tessa, the housemaid, left, you remember her? Then Bessie, the parlor maid quit, so there was no one to use the rooms up in the servants' quarters. Nothin' up there but the attic for storage."

I picked up the spoon automatically and dipped it into the mound of porridge. But my mind was whirling. I felt a new chill that had nothing to do with my long walk in the dampness. If nobody lived above the third floor anymore, what were all those sounds I'd heard at night? Tricks the wind played blowing through the nooks, crevices, and crannies of this weird old house?

"Why don't the new help Aunt Octavia hired live in?"

Lutie shrugged. "None of the girls she interviewed would agree to stay."

"That's odd. I'm sure Aunt Octavia pays as good a wage as anyone else. Why can't she get live-in help?" I had my own ideas, but I wanted to hear Lutie's.

"Well, miss, nobody comes right out and says so —" Lutie paused while she picked up two quilted potholders and carefully brought a pan of pecan-studded cinnamon rolls out of the oven — "but my sister tells me, it's *her* opinion, mind you, that it's because Woodvale people have an idea Octagon House is — haunted."

"Haunted?"

"Haunted," she confirmed. "I don't know

when the stories got started; I didn't hear any until after Mrs. Henshaw left. Tessa had left before that, lives over in Perrysville now. But there was talk of strange moving lights circling in the night, and some claimed to have seen a ghost in the cupola!" Lutie wagged her head, saying, "It was all a lot of nonsense, but you know how people like to talk. Gossip spreads." She brushed her hands together, dusting them off as if finished with the subject, and said, "Anyway, since then they've never been able to get any help to stay overnight."

Right then the back door burst open, letting in a blast of cold air, and Miss Ingersoll, bundled in a heavy mackintosh and wearing men's boots, came stomping inside. Seeing me sitting at the kitchen table, she forced a smile and said briskly, "Had my morning constitutional. Temperature's dropping. We may get some snow before the week's up. I'll be back for Miss Octavia's breakfast tray, Lutie," she tossed back over her shoulder as she pushed through the swinging door and disappeared. Lutie rolled her eyes upward, silently expressing her feelings about the nurse.

I finished my coffee but left most of my oatmeal; I just wasn't hungry. Then I wandered down the front hall and looked in the dining room and then the drawing room to see if either Toby or Elvira was down. But both rooms were empty, so I started upstairs. Just as I rounded the landing to the third floor, I met Elvira coming down. She was dressed to go out, wearing a stylish suit of beige cashmere, a set of stone marten furs draped around her shoulders. Her bonnet was a dashing concoction of brown velvet ribboned in faille bows.

"*You* look quite gorgeous!" I declared in playful awe. "You'll set Woodvale on its heels!" I teased.

Elvira didn't smile, but just glared as she pulled on brown kid gloves. "I don't think this is a time to try and be funny, Julie," she said severely as she carefully smoothed each finger. "If you refuse to take this — this dilemma we're in *seriously*, then *one* of us has to. Toby seems quite incapable of doing so, and as a result, I guess it is up to me to look after *all* our interests. Tell Lutie that I won't be here for lunch," she said as she swept by me down the stairs.

What was Elvira up to now? I wondered.

The door of Toby's room, down the hall from mine, was shut, and no sound came from there. I supposed he was sleeping off the result of emptying the sherry decanter the night before. I went on to my own room.

With Elvira off on her mysterious under-taking and Toby "incommunicado" for the next several hours, why not accept Jordan's offer to go with him over to Perrysville? I thought. He had mentioned stopping for dinner on the way back. It was tempting.

It would be a welcome alternative to the oppressiveness of Octagon House, besides giving us the chance for a real talk as he had suggested. A kind of tremor went through me, half excitement, half dread. Could our relationship be restored? Or was it just that the present situation was so intolerable and my own future so uncertain that I was putting too much into this outing with Jordan?

For the rest of the morning I debated the wisdom of going. In the end I decided the only way to get answers to some of these be-wildering questions was to see Jordan again.

As I changed into my sensible dark blue traveling suit, I almost wished I could borrow one of Elvira's elegant ensembles. I did have a pretty blouse of dusty-rose taf-feta, with an embroidered yoke and tiny appliqued flowers on the bodice and sleeves. It would "fancy up" my outfit a little. My bonnet, which I'd bought on a whim, was becoming, with its cluster of redbuds nes-tled among dark green velvet leaves.

As I examined myself critically in the mirror, I stuck out my tongue at my image. Why was I taking such pains with my appearance? Perhaps I was building false hopes about Jordan. Possibly the chance of a renewed romance was just an illusion. Anxiously I debated another minute, then asked myself what I had to lose by going. So adjusting the angle of my bonnet, I hurried downstairs and on my way.

But when I reached the gray-shingle house that had been Dr. Hugh Barret's — and where Jordan now lived — I hesitated a split second before opening the white picket gate and walking up to the front door.

In answer to my knock a pleasant-faced, gray-haired woman in a neat plum-colored dress with lace collars and cuffs opened the door. "There are no office hours today, miss; Doctor has to go to Perrysville," she began, then stopped, put her head to one side for a second, then apologized. "Oh, I'm sorry, miss. You're Miss Julie Madison, aren't you? Doctor told me he was expecting a guest, I do beg your pardon. Please come in. I'm Mrs. Hammond, the housekeeper. Doctor isn't here at the moment, but he should be directly."

I stepped inside and immediately felt a welcoming warmth, an atmosphere much in contrast to Octagon House. Mrs. Hammond led the way into a low-ceilinged room, cozy with a mixture of chintz-covered furniture. A bright fire burned merrily in a raised stone fireplace, and braided rugs were scattered on the mellow pine floor.

"Could I offer you a cup of tea, miss?"

"No, thank you," I said.

"Well, then, we'll just sit and have a nice chat until Doctor comes." And she motioned me to take a seat on the curved love seat near the fire. By her easy manner I could tell Mrs. Hammond was an old and trusted family employee. I discovered she was quite garrulous as well.

"Doctor should be returning any minute, but then, you just never know. He was called out on an emergency." She paused, then said, "Actually, it was up to Octagon House he went, miss."

Alarmed, I asked, "To Octagon House? On an emergency? Was it my aunt? Something serious?"

The housekeeper looked prim, shook her head slightly, and said, "To tell you the truth, miss, it's not all that unusual. Being called up to Octagon House that is. *On an emergency,*" she added with emphasis. "No offense, miss, but I think your aunt is a bit of a hypochondriac. She did the same thing with the old doctor, Dr. Hugh, Dr. Jordan's uncle. And he would drop everything and rush right up there, no matter what time of day or night. Sometimes he'd just stepped in the house, ready to drop from fatigue, and here would come the driver from Octagon House. An emergency, indeed. Begging your pardon, miss, but it's my opinion Miss Vale creates her own emergency whenever it suits her fancy."

Mrs. Hammond folded her arms and continued. "I used to tell Dr. Hugh, and I tell Dr. Jordan now, why should he go dashing up there on her every notion? Let his nice dinner get stone-cold half the time? But Dr. Hugh paid no attention. He'd try to pacify me with a joke. 'I have to go, Mrs. Hammond, or Miss Vale will cut me out of her will!' he'd say. Oh, Dr. Hugh was quite a joker." She smiled reminiscently. "Of course, Dr. Jordan is more serious. But, still, when Miss Vale calls, he jumps. Just like his uncle did. I teased him one day, quoting Dr. Hugh: 'What's the matter, Dr. Jordan, you afraid Miss Vale will cut you out of her will?' "

I didn't know why — maybe it was all this talk of wills reminding me of last night and the disturbing discussion with Elvira — but

Mrs. Hammond's recital sent a shiver of distaste all through me.

For some reason I began to feel uneasy. Maybe it hadn't been such a good idea for me to come over here to meet Jordan, to plan to spend the afternoon and early evening with him. Maybe it would be better not to try to resurrect the past, revive old feelings. Maybe it was as bad a mistake to come here as it had been to return to Woodvale and to Octagon House.

Something of what I was thinking must have shown in my face because I saw Mrs. Hammond looking at me curiously, her eyes squinting behind her small, oval spectacles.

I half-rose from my seat, an excuse to leave forming on my lips, but before I could speak, the front door opened and there stood Jordan, tall, handsome, smiling, regarding me in a way that made me draw in my breath and made my heart trip astonishingly.

Chapter Twelve

"I have only a few patients to see over here, so it I shouldn't take too long," Jordan said as we drove into Perrysville. "Most of them are elderly and lonely, so I usually spend a little time just talking to them rather than doing any real 'doctoring.' That's as much of a tonic to them as anything I could prescribe. Do you think you can find enough to amuse yourself while I make my house calls?"

"Oh, yes, I'm sure I can, Jordan. Don't worry about me. I love browsing in art galleries and bookstores and antique shops."

"You'll find all that here even though Perrysville is pretty quiet now in the winter. In the summer the sidewalks are so crowded with tourists you can hardly move. Luckily, the inn stays open year-round. I thought we could have dinner there."

Jordan turned in at the livery stable, where one of the young boys came running out to take his horse's head.

"Howdy, Dr. Barret," the boy greeted him.

"Hello there, Jim," Jordan answered. Then he turned to me. "I shouldn't be over an hour and a half, maybe two hours at the most. If you get tired window-shopping, just go to the inn and wait for me there. They have a nice sitting room, where you'll be warm and comfortable. How does that sound?"

"Fine," I agreed.

Jordan got his black medical bag from the back of the buggy, and we walked together to the street corner, where we parted.

I had always loved coming over to Perrysville even as a child. It was right on the coast; in the old days it was mainly a fishing village. Gradually it had developed into an artists' colony, then a popular family summer vacation spot. It had a wonderful white sand beach and dear little carpenter Gothic cottages lined up on the dunes overlooking the ocean. Of course, on a winter day like this, with its chill wind and overcast sky, it had a deserted look.

I started strolling down the one main street. Many of the stores were boarded up and closed. I found only a few open; all of them had a somnambulant appearance. In the window of the Book Nook a yellow striped tabby cat was curled asleep. At the art gallery I thought I'd go inside, but when I tried the door, I found it was locked, and I saw a small lettered sign that said OUT TO LUNCH. Since it was nearly four, I guessed they were probably gone for the day.

Farther down the street I saw a wooden sign that said ANTIQUES swinging in the brisk wind, and I headed toward it. Stopping to look in the window before going inside, I got a shock.

I stared unbelieving at the display in the window. There before my eyes was the very thing I had sensed was missing from the drawing room at Octagon House. I hadn't been able to remember then what it was. But now I saw it. The pair of porcelain dogs!

I had always thought they were hideous with their ugly, flattened faces and tongues sticking out maliciously. How could I have forgotten them? Every time I had been called into the drawing room to face a sarcastic tongue-lashing from Aunt Octavia, I had focused my attention on them to keep from crying. Whether it was a lecture over a poor report card or some infraction of the strict house rules she laid down for us, I would concentrate on those implacable dogs, sitting there, impervious to any human frailty or emotion.

I remembered the frustration I felt that first night back at Octagon House when the memory of what was missing eluded me. But I would know these pieces anywhere. So what were they doing in a Perrysville antique shop?

Cautiously I pushed open the door and stepped inside. The tinkling sound of the overhead bell alerted the woman in the back of the shop to the arrival of a customer. She nodded and smiled, then said, "Good afternoon, is there anything special I can help you find? Or would you rather just have a look around yourself?"

"Yes, thank you," I murmured. I thought it best not to question her immediately about the twin dogs. I wasn't sure why, but some instinct warned me to wait. I circled the small store slowly, pausing here and there to lift up some item and examine it as though considering it for purchase.

There was a variety of things for sale, some genuine antiques, others merely attractive or unusual oddities. None as valuable as I knew the porcelain dogs to be.

How had Aunt Octavia's prized china canines come to be here? Of course, I could be mistaken. There were probably other sets of such dogs. Still, I was curious to find out where they had come from if I could.

After I felt I'd browsed long enough, I sauntered back to where the woman was polishing glassware and asked with elaborate casualness, "How much are those strange-looking dog statues in the window?"

"Oh, *them*. Now, they're *real* antiques. Some of our things are not that special. But *those* come from a home that's filled with very fine objets d'art." She very carefully pronounced the words "obayjays days art." as though she had been tutored to do so.

She put down the hobnail pitcher she'd been shining and warily moved through the maze of tables laden with delicate collectibles over to the display window. She reached in and picked up one of the dogs, brought it back to me, and turned it upside down so I could see the hallmark.

Lowering her voice, as if to give the information more significance, she told me, "These were brought in for the owner by an agent and placed here on consignment. We always protect the name of the consignee in cases like this because — as the agent said — the owner would *never* have parted with them except for dire financial necessity. We treat such matters with absolute confidentiality. However, I can assure you, based upon other things we have taken and sold from this same source, that this is the *gen-u-ine* article. Very old, very valuable."

I was positive it was one of those missing from Aunt Octavia's mantelpiece. Looking from the dog she was holding into the woman's eyes, I saw they were as honest as I had ever encountered. If there was anything underhanded about these antiques being put up for sale here, I was convinced she had nothing to do with it. But who did? And why?

As we looked at each other, I realized there was something endearingly familiar about the plump, earnest face. Was it possible?

She was ten years older and thirty pounds heavier, but I felt sure this was the delightful housemaid who had protected and defended us often, covering up for us, smuggling food up to us in our rooms when we had been sent to bed without supper!

I trusted my intuition and asked tentatively, "Are you — Tessa?"

"Yes, I'm Tessa, but who — ?"

"Did you used to be housemaid at Octagon House in Woodvale?"

Bewilderment clouded her face for a split second, followed by gradual recognition, then amazement. "Yes!" she exclaimed. "And you are — ? Oh, no! Could it be? Is it really you? *Miss Julie!*"

I nodded vigorously. "Yes, Tessa, I'm Julie Madison, Miss Vale's niece."

"Oh, my stars! I can't believe it!" she gasped. "It must be at least ten years since I left there, and you must have been — what, thirteen?" A wide smile replaced her look of astonished recognition. "What are you doing in Perrysville? I thought all you children left Octagon House years ago."

"We did. I've been gone nearly six years. I'm just over here for the afternoon. I've been visiting at Octagon House; our aunt sent for all of us, Elvira, Toby, and me. We're all there," I told her.

At once her face fell and took on a look of sympathy. "Sure, I was sorry to hear about the old lady, even though she was a bit of a tyrant when I worked there. But I'm never happy to hear about anyone coming on hard times," Tessa said.

"Yes, her health is bad and she has aged," I agreed.

"I wasn't talking about her health so much. All of us will be old if we live long enough, I always say." Tessa lowered her voice. "I mean her fortune. Sad to think a family who practically built and owned a town like Woodvale would come to such straits."

"I don't know what you mean, Tessa," I said, puzzled.

133

"Oh, its fair common knowledge, miss," Tessa whispered. "I'm not much one for gossip."

My shock must have shown and I protested, "I had no idea. I've seen no evidence of any problem since I've been at Octagon House."

"I'm sure they want to keep a good face on it, miss."

I was trying to absorb this startling information. I wanted to find out how Tessa happened to be involved in this store and get her back on the subject of the china dogs that had been placed here on consignment. But I wasn't sure how without telling her what I suspected.

"Are you the owner here?" I asked.

"No, miss, I just work here part-time. It helps out during the winter months because my husband's a logger, and he can't work in the woods this time of year. And I enjoy working around pretty things, talking to people that comes in and all."

"Then, I suppose it's the owner who deals with confidential placements of such things as these dogs?" I tried to sound casual.

"Oh, yes, and he's very secretive about it, he is. He keeps all the records locked up; I don't know who brings things in to sell. Mr. Carmody goes out to people's houses that wants to sell things, appraises them, then gives them a price he feels he can get for them, and of course, he takes a commission. In the summer time wealthy people from Boston and New York come up here, and they don't seem to care what they pay for things, miss!" Tessa shook her head.

I handed her back the china dog I'd been holding. I could be wrong about them, I told myself, but intuitively I felt they had once been at Octagon House, my aunt's possessions. Was the rumor about her true? Was she selling off some of her valuable antiques?

Suddenly I realized I'd spent quite a bit of time here, and I didn't want to be late meeting Jordan, so I started to the door. But I didn't want to leave without purchasing something. I spotted a small brass paperweight in the shape of a shepherd boy seated on a tree stump playing the flute, two lambs at his bare feet. It was quaint and quite charming, and I asked Tessa the price.

The amount she named was really more than I wanted to pay, but since I was in such a hurry, I said I'd take it.

"It's solid brass, miss, and the only one of its kind we've ever got in," she told me as she took it over to the counter to wrap it and ring up the sale. "Well, it was certainly a surprise to see you, Miss Julie." She shook her head as if she still couldn't believe it. "I'm glad you stopped by."

I wasn't so sure *I* was! I was now in the possession of some unsettling suspicions as well as a paperweight I didn't want and had no use for. But I tried to smile at Tessa and murmured something pleasant about being happy to see her again, too.

"Tell Lutie hello for me, won't you, miss?" she called after me as I opened the door and started out. I assured her I would.

Disconcerted by my confused thoughts, I hurried toward the town square. I was completely baffled. What was going on at Octagon House? Aunt Octavia talking about hundreds of thousands of dollars in the estate to be managed on one hand, and on the other hand, selling her family's valuable artifacts — was she getting senile? Did she not know what she was doing? Should I ask Jordan about my aunt's mental state?

I felt that something sinister was going on and I found that very frightening. There was so much hidden at Octagon House, so many secrets, one could not be sure what the truth was. A web of secrecy surrounded Octagon House and its occupants, and it was drawing me in, tightening around me, binding me ever more closely and possibly cutting off any chance of escape.

Chapter Thirteen

I was thoroughly chilled by the time I met Jordan, either from nerves or from the wind that had risen sharply. Jordan was just going up the steps of the inn as I came around the corner.

The Stagecoach Inn was a large, rambling clapboard and native stone building, restored and refurbished from the old days when it had actually been the only stop for weary travelers between Boston and these remote little New England towns.

The minute we stepped inside I felt embraced by its warmth and charm. Colonial furniture filled the room. Primitive portraits and framed hand-drawn early maps decorated the walls, and an antique musket hung over the rough stone fireplace, all adding to the inn's delightful ambience. A waitress dressed in a ruffled mopcap and calico dress showed us to a table near the fireplace.

Sitting opposite Jordan in the candlelit dining room, it was hard to imagine how upset I had been earlier. The glowing fire burning in the corner fireplace and the hot mulled cider Jordan ordered for us seemed to lull my disquieting thoughts.

"I was afraid I'd be late meeting you. One of my patients has an endless stream of minor complaints as well as stories to tell me. It was hard to get away." Jordan smiled ruefully. "I'm glad I didn't keep you waiting. You must have enjoyed your shopping. Did you find anything interesting?"

I started to confide my startling discovery, then wondering if I should, I hesitated, and as I did, the waitress brought our menus. The next few minutes were taken up with deciding what to eat. After that it seemed useless to mention something I could not prove. Besides, I did not want to break the pleasant, relaxed mood by bringing up troubling subjects.

We ate dinner in a companionable manner. I found I was surprisingly hungry, and I enjoyed every bite. As I finished I said, "Thank you for bringing me out, Jordan. This is just what I needed." I sighed as I added, "It's been dreadful at Octagon House ever since Aunt Octavia announced her plan about the estate. Elvira's been impossible, Toby morose, everyone under such tremendous pressure."

Jordan frowned as he asked, "Julie, are you sure you understood Miss Octavia correctly? Is she actually going to *change* her will or let it stand as it now is and just name one of you as executor?"

"I believe she means to *change* the will so that only *one* person inherits *everything*. Then, at that person's discretion everything else will be decided. That's what has Elvira so enraged. For some reason she believes — and Toby seems to agree with her — that the original will divided everything up between all the surviving heirs. The children of Clement Vale by his *first* wife, who are Aunt Octavia and Uncle Victor, and *our* parents, who are the children of his second marriage. Elvira claims that since each of us lost our Vale parent, *we* should inherit their share of the estate. Now Aunt Octavia means to change all that because *she* is the executrix of her father *and* stepmother's estate and has power of attorney to do whatever she wants."

Jordan's frown deepened. "So, if Toby or Elvira or *you* is chosen as the sole inheritor, the original will can be ignored and everything redivided, right?"

"Yes. But, Jordan, I don't plan to accept even if by some stretch of the imagination Aunt Octavia designates me, which, of course, she won't!"

"What do you mean?"

"Simply that I want no part of Octagon House. I've always associated it with great unhappiness — with tragedy. We three came there as half-orphans; each of our Vale parents died young and tragically. Elvira's father was presumably a reckless, irresponsible rogue. He died in an amateur buggy racing accident. Her mother had to go back on the stage to support her until finally she was forced to send her to Octagon House. We were never directly told, but we *think* Toby's father died under questionable circumstances. And my mother died in a train accident — ironically, on her way back to Woodvale, to Octagon House, at the request of Aunt Octavia, because Grandmother Vale was supposed to be dying!" Involuntarily I shuddered at the memory.

Jordan reached over and covered my hand with his. "Sorry, Julie, maybe I shouldn't have brought this up. But you seemed so troubled, I thought it might help to talk about it."

His eyes, looking at me with such sincere sympathy, touched me, and again I started to tell him my suspicions about the china dogs in the antique shop. Then something peculiar happened that stopped me.

Jordan pulled out his watch and consulted

140

it. I saw that it was a handsome gold one on a woven chain, hardly the kind you'd expect a country doctor to wear.

"I'm afraid we'll have to start back, Julie. I still have to make hospital rounds tonight," he said regretfully. Then, seeing my eyes on his watch, a smile touched his mouth briefly. "You should never play poker, Julie. Your face is a giveaway. You're wondering about my watch, aren't you?" he asked.

I had the grace to blush.

"Let me read you the inscription," he continued in spite of my embarrassment. " 'To Jordan Barret on the occasion of his graduation from medical school, June 1895. OV.' Do you know what those initials stand for? Octavia Vale. It was a gift from your aunt," he said as he replaced the watch in his vest pocket.

Jordan got to his feet and came behind my chair. He placed both his hands on my shoulders for a brief moment. I felt something quiver through me at his touch. Then he drew back the chair and assisted me into my suit jacket and cape.

When we walked out onto the porch of the inn, a light, misty rain was falling. The young fellow from the livery stable had brought Jordan's horse and buggy around and was waiting for us in front. Jordan helped me in, and we started back to Wood-vale.

Neither of us had much to say on the way. All at once I was drained of energy and the desire to initiate conversation. I had so much on my mind. So much had happened in the few days I'd been back in Woodvale, and all of it confusing. Most of all, my feelings about Jordan were mixed. I remembered how casually he had mentioned the call on Aunt Octavia that had delayed our trip, the one his housekeeper had called an emergency. What was his ambivalent relationship to Aunt Octavia? Who was Jordan Barret now? I didn't know. Against the rhythmic *clip-clop* of the horse's hooves on the wet cobblestones came some troubling questions.

"Do you mind if I make a stop at the pharmacy?" Jordan asked as we passed the Woodvale city limits. "I have to get some chemicals Don Martin ordered for me. I make up my own prescriptions most of the time. It makes it simpler if I do it right on the spot when I make my diagnosis, instead of sending over to him all the time, especially when I'm out in the country on a house call."

"No, I don't mind, Jordan," I said, and he pulled up in front of the Woodvale Pharmacy. I was certainly in no hurry to go back to Octagon House.

"This won't take long," Jordan promised.

My eyes followed his tall figure through the pharmacy door. I wished I did not have so many doubts about him, about his motives. I'd been so in love with him once. Could I be again? Or had we both changed too much? And underneath all those questions lurked one I did not even want to admit was there. Could I really trust Jordan?

The rain was coming down harder and faster now. Through the spattered eisenglass windows of the buggy I could see the street and sidewalks, shiny slick in the light from the lampposts. Downtown was practically deserted. That was why the solitary figure of a man coming up the sidewalk caught my attention. His head was bent, shoulders hunched into his upturned coat collar.

There was something familiar about him. I sat up straighter, peering through the rain-smeared window. Then, when he stopped under the streetlight, waiting for a carriage to pass before crossing the street, I recognized the thatch of reddish hair! Toby! It was Toby! What was he doing downtown at this hour on this beastly night?

I did not have long to guess, for as soon as

the street was clear, he hurried across, heading straight for Woodvale Tavern. I watched as he pushed through the door and disappeared.

Oh, Toby, I thought with a trace of sadness. I hated the knowledge that my cousin was so directionless in his life. If Aunt Octavia named him sole inheritor, would he straighten up and live up to his potential? He *was* the only male, as he had pointed out, the only one of we three who carried the Vale name —

"Sorry to be so long." Jordan's voice broke into my thoughts as he climbed back in the buggy. He put a package behind the buggy seat, then picked up the reins, and we were on our way again.

As we started up the hill leading to Octagon House, Jordan said, "It's been really wonderful being with you again today, Julie. We must find a way to spend more time together. There are still things we need to discuss —"

"Jordan, I don't know how long I'll be here. I plan to talk to Aunt Octavia and tell her I refuse to be considered as sole inheritor —"

"I hope you're not serious, Julie. I hope you won't do anything as foolish as that," Jordan interrupted. "I mean, that's a big decision to make so quickly. You said you had to talk to Elvira and Toby, and I advise you to talk to a lawyer as well — the Vale estate is, well, a very large one. A person could do much good with that amount of money —" He halted, and then his tone of voice changed. "Maybe I'm being selfish, but I'm afraid if you decide not to be considered as the inheritor, you'll leave — and our second chance will be gone."

Holding the reins with one hand, he reached over and took one of mine. "I would like to try to see if things can work out for us — wouldn't you, Julie? That is, unless there is someone else you haven't told me about, someone else you care for . . . ?"

I thought of Francis Wilburn, the widowed history professor for whom I'd done research at the college where my father taught, who had asked me to marry him. Although there had been others who might have been interested in me, I'd discouraged any serious attention. Francis was the only one I'd even considered. But in the end even he had not been able to erase Jordan's image from my secret heart, and I had, gently, I hoped, turned him down.

"No, Jordan, there isn't anyone," I answered truthfully.

"Then, don't make any rash decisions

Julie. Don't leave. Please don't." His voice was intense.

"I don't know, Jordan, I'm not sure. . . ." I said hesitantly.

At this he jerked on the reins, abruptly pulling the buggy to the side of the road and braking it. He turned and took me into his arms. "What do I have to say or do to convince you, Julie?" he asked, and then he kissed me. I felt his lips move over my mouth, and it parted under his insistence. With his kiss a flame of remembrance rushed through my body, bringing back all the sweetness of past kisses, all the ardor of first love. But this kiss held more than I remembered. This was a man's kiss, full of passion and longing and desire.

Chapter Fourteen

I was still dazed with my newly awakened emotions as I came into the house, still felt the warmth of Jordan's kiss on my mouth, was still elated by the sensations it had aroused in me. But the minute I stepped inside the door, I felt a palpable oppressiveness. It was as if a heavy cloak had dropped over me.

No one was anywhere downstairs. A lamp left burning on the hall table under Grandfather Vale's portrait gave me the disconcerting impression that the old gentleman was slyly amused at the trouble his will was causing his descendants.

I turned away quickly and started upstairs. I had just reached the third-floor landing when a figure rushed toward me out of the shadows. Thin fingers closed on my upper arm in a viselike grip!

Elvira! Evidently she had been standing behind the balustrade.

"Come in here," she hissed, dragging me with her down the hall. She pushed me into her bedroom, then followed quickly, shutting the door behind us.

"There's been the most beastly row!" she whispered. "Between Aunt Octavia and Toby. I heard every word," she declared. At my accusing look she said defensively, "I couldn't avoid it! They were both shouting."

"Sit down," she ordered, pointing to her bed. I sat.

"I had no idea about Toby, did you?" she asked. "I mean, it seems he's mishandled his life pretty badly. He certainly has bungled his chances with Aunt Octavia."

"For heaven's sake, Elvira, are you going to tell me what happened or not?"

"Well, as you know," she began, "I went downtown today. I wanted to make some investigations on my own as to the precise status of the Vale estate. It took much longer than I expected. I had to look up records in the county court house. Then I tried to get an appointment with Ross Holden, Aunt Octavia's lawyer. But they told me he was out of the office." She leaned closer, lowering her voice conspiratorily. "I found out later he was *here!* Closeted with Aunt Octavia all afternoon! Of course, it's about the will and —"

"Please, Elvira, tell me about Toby!" I pleaded, exasperated.

Elvira shot me an indignant glance. "Well, you *should* be just as interested in what I found out today — it concerns *you* as much as it does me or Toby!" Elvira frowned. "I went to talk to some real estate people, tried to find out what property goes for now around here, how much uncut timberlands are worth — that sort of thing —"

"About Toby, Elvira!" I persisted.

"Well, all right, I got home late in the afternoon. Toby was in the drawing room, already at the sherry — as you might imagine! I tried to discuss some of the information I'd gathered and what I thought the three of us should do — but in the middle of our conversation Marshall appeared and told Toby that Aunt Octavia wanted to see him."

She paused, nervously biting her lips. "Toby attempted to make a joke about it to me. Remarked that it must be his turn before the Inquisitor or his Day of Judgment — some words to that effect. Anyway, he went up to Aunt Octavia's suite, and I went up to my room thinking I'd lie down for a while before dinner."

"So? What about Toby and Aunt Octavia?" I prodded.

"I couldn't nap; I was too excited about all the information I'd garnered this afternoon, and then I heard voices. I got up and went to my door and opened it." She gave me another defensive look. "You would have done the same thing if you'd heard all that, too. I went and leaned over the banister, and I could see that Aunt Octavia's door was open and Toby was standing there. Of course, neither of them could see *me*" — she lifted her thin shoulders in a shrug — "there was no way for me *not* to hear what they were saying —"

"What *was* it, Elvira?" I was nearly at the end of my patience.

"I can repeat it almost word for word! 'Wastrel! Ne'er-do-well! Do you actually think I haven't kept track of you all these years? I had such high hopes for you. You were so talented, had such promise! But you are weak, just like your father! No willpower, no fortitude, no character! His weakness was alcohol! Yours is gambling!' " Here Elvira wagged her finger furiously in an uncanny imitation of our aunt when angered. " 'Oh, yes, I know all about the money you threw away, just as you threw away your talent! Do you think I would send money year after year and never know how it was spent? When the conservatory wrote that your tuition bills weren't paid, I started checking.' " Elvira put her hands on her hips and leaned toward me just as I'd seen Aunt

150

Octavia do dozens of times. " 'I hired a private investigator to follow you! Ha! Perhaps you didn't think your dotty old aunt would know about such things, but I am more intelligent than you may have guessed.'

"I was shocked. I couldn't believe even Aunt Octavia would have him followed. She just kept on and on at him. 'I know much more about your life when you were supposed to be pursuing your musical education. I know about the shoddy little affairs — the last one was when I cut off the funds! It was the last straw.'

"I swear it's true Julie, I'm *not* exaggerating. Then she said, 'I gave you chance after chance, blaming your youth, your inexperience after the sheltered childhood you had here at Octagon House. But at last even my lenience came to an end. I found out about all the shabby tricks you played, working on my sympathies, trying to get me to send more money on any pretext you could devise. But I'm no fool, Toby, nor senile!' " Elvira's face twisted sardonically into a mask remarkably resembling our Aunt's. " 'It's settled. You'll not get a penny more from me. You have already received *your* inheritance, Toby. You have proved yourself untrustworthy, undeserving. I am not the righteous father of the Bible, you can be sure of that, Toby; I don't forgive that easily. You're finished as far as the Vale estate is concerned.' "

Elvira's voice had taken on all the scathing venom of Aunt Octavia's imitating her to the letter.

Hearing Aunt Octavia's cruel, wounding words, instant compassion for Toby swept over me. How awful that must have been for him. No wonder he was seeking oblivion in drink at the Woodvale Tavern.

"Did you hear me, Julie?" Elvira's voice sharply jerked me back from my sympathetic thoughts for Toby.

"Yes, Elvira, I heard you." I sighed. "Poor Toby."

"Yes, of course," Elvira agreed quickly. "But do you realize what this means? *This* means that it's now between you and me, Julie. It's one of *us* that Aunt Octavia means to name sole inheritor," she said with an air of triumph that seemed deplorable under the circumstances.

I stared at my cousin. There was an excited gleam in her eyes, unmistakable avarice. I seemed to be looking at a stranger. What I saw in her expression frightened me. It was greed, raw and ugly.

Unaware of my reaction, Elvira proceeded in a voice that almost shook with excitement. "Julie, we're talking about an estate worth far more than I had ever dreamed. And we all can have a piece of the pie. Since Aunt Octavia has now ruled Toby out, we must agree on a plan that will benefit us all, *including* Toby. Aunt Octavia will never even have to know. She can't live forever, and even if she holds on to everything until she dies, the person who inherits — one of *us* would certainly not want to live in this mausoleum of a house!" Elvira's voice rose with mounting eagerness as she outlined her strategy. "Therefore, I suggest that whoever is named sole inheritor sell off a certain amount of land, which should bring in a sizable amount. Cash! Then the two who have been left out can at least have a portion of their share of the entire estate — and I assure you from what I learned today, the amount will be generous. When Aunt Octavia *does* die, well, then the three of us can decide on the division of the rest of the property. Doesn't that seem fair?"

I must have looked blank, for she rushed on. "We'd do this right away, as soon as Aunt Octavia makes her decision, which she said was going to be while we were all here. So, as I said before, none of us will leave here empty-handed."

"Of course, I *assume* you don't intend to

share this — this plan of yours with Aunt Octavia?" I asked.

Elvira did not seem to catch the sarcasm that had crept into my tone.

"Certainly not. After one of us takes over, *she* won't have anything more to say about anything."

I got up off the bed and started toward the door.

"Why are you leaving?" she asked.

"I don't want to talk about this anymore, Elvira."

I wanted no part of a counterconspiracy. Witnessing what my childhood companion had become sickened me.

"Well, all right, Julie," Elvira retorted indignantly. "But tomorrow we'll know which one of *us* it's going to be. And I thought you'd want to know what I suggest is best for the sole inheritor to do —"

"Good night, Elvira," I said, cutting her off as she was starting in on the whole thing again.

I made my way down the hall to my own bedroom. All I wanted to do was be alone and hope for the blankness of sleep. The atmosphere of this house was threatening to infect everyone with selfishness and subterfuge. Was that our heritage from Aunt Octavia?

I felt drained and weary. My main emotion was an urgent wish to escape from Octagon House entirely.

But then I thought about Jordan. I had promised him to give us a chance, hadn't I? If I left, I owed him some explanation. I'd send him a note. Impulsively I sat down at the little desk where I used to do my homework, drew out some stationery, dipped the pen into the inkwell, and began to write rapidly. At first I poured out all my pent-up feelings about coming back to Woodvale, seeing him, about Aunt Octavia's devious plan, my disappointment in my cousins, about him and a possible future. Then I stopped. I'd said too much. It wasn't safe to write down all these intimate thoughts. I pushed the pages I'd written away without rereading them. I was sure they were incoherent. I got out more paper and began another note. This time I got little further than "Dear Jordan." Each attempt to explain myself was worse than the last. Three scribbled pages later I tossed everything I'd written into the wastepaper basket. I'd just started again when a low, furtive tap came at my door.

I controlled a groan. Hoping it wasn't Elvira, I went over to the door and opened it. It was Toby.

My mouth opened to say his name, and he quickly put his forefinger to his lips, indicating silence. Then, mouthing the words, "I need to talk to you," he beckoned me out into the hall and along toward the stairway. Mystified, I followed him, tiptoeing after him down the two flights of steps to the first floor and into the small parlor. He did not speak until he had closed the doors.

"Have you talked to Elvira tonight?" he asked in a stage whisper.

I nodded.

"Then you've heard her little scheme." He smiled and shook his head.

"Yes, and I've also heard about your conversation with Aunt Octavia."

"Conversation? I wouldn't call it *that* exactly!" He gave a short laugh. "More like the reading of the riot act. Not that I didn't deserve it." He walked over and held up a bottle of brandy. "Look what I discovered in the unlocked wine cabinet. I wanted you to join me."

The last thing I wanted was a brandy. I tried preventing him by saying "Haven't you had enough, Toby? I saw you go into the Woodvale Tavern earlier this evening."

He looked at me reproachfully. "A walk back here in the freezing rain sobered me up fast. It's begun to sleet." Then he asked,

"How did you happen to see me?"

I told him, and he shrugged. "I only had a few beers there. Come on, Julie, this is the time for midnight confidences in front of the fire."

"All right," I said, coming over to the fireplace and sitting down.

He had already filled two brandy snifters with amber liquid and now gave one to me. Then he sat down opposite me.

"Since you've already received a blow by blow description from Elvira about what happened, I'll just start by telling you most of what Aunt Octavia said was true. My first reaction to her diatribe was to leave — I mean *really* — not just Octagon House, but Woodvale. I even walked as far as the train station, but the last train out of here had left. That's how I happened to end up at the Woodvale Tavern. While I was there, I got to thinking about Elvira's scheme, and I thought, why not? Why not stick around and see how the game plays out."

I made no comment, just took a sip of the brandy and felt its sweet burning smoothness slide down my throat.

Toby swirled his around before taking a swallow. "I don't know about you, Julie, but I could really use cash and soon. I'm up to here in debt —" He made a slicing gesture across his neck with one hand — "I've run out of friends I can borrow from, and I don't have a job to go back to. In fact, my purpose in coming up here was to see if I could get Aunt Octavia to advance me some money." He lowered his head, looking ashamed, but struggled on. "I even thought of cashing in the train ticket she sent me to get some quick money. Then I decided I might do better if I came in person. I'm not proud of this, Julie, but I'd even made up a story I was going to use to try to convince her — that I needed an operation on my hand." He held up his hand, flexing blunt-tipped fingers. "A real rotter, eh?"

I didn't know what to say, so I murmured, "Sometimes, as the poet says, desperate times require desperate measures. Sounds to me like you were desperate, Toby."

"Ah, Julie, you're a softy." He smiled at me. "But I can, at least, be honest about myself. Well, it's all in the toss, I guess. I gambled and lost. I've never been afraid to put all my cards on the table, play all my chips, win or lose. This time I lost." He finished his brandy. "I'll just stick around to see which of you fair ladies wins the prize."

"Not me, Toby. I've told you and Elvira —" I protested.

"Can't you think of anything you could

do with two hundred thousand dollars, Julie?" Toby leveled his eyes on me. "That's approximately what selling off a few acres of Vale property would bring; didn't Elvira inform you of that little figure?"

The accumulation of physical tiredness and emotional turmoil descended upon me. The day had been filled with startling revelations, unsolved puzzles, secret plans, and hidden motives, and I suddenly felt overburdened. I put down my nearly empty glass and said, "I can't even think any more tonight, Toby. I have to go to bed." I stood up, swaying a little. Holding on to the arm of the chair, I told him, "I'm sorry, Toby, about what happened with Aunt Octavia — sorry about your financial straits — everything. But I can't — *we* can't — do anything about it tonight."

"It's all right, Julie. I guess I just needed to tell someone. You always were a good listener." He rose and put an arm around my shoulder and walked with me to the door. "By the way, my time at Woodvale Tavern wasn't a total loss. I picked up some interesting information." He chuckled. "I was talking to the bartender, and when he heard I was visiting at Octagon House, he told me a chap from here was a 'regular.' Now, who do you suppose *that* would be?"

159

"I don't know. Not *Marshall?*"

"From the description I'd hazard a good bet on it. Then one of the barmaids came up and overheard us talking, and added a juicy tidbit of gossip — she said he usually met a woman there, and they went into a booth to talk."

"A woman? Marshall? I *am* surprised. Who do you suppose it is?"

"The barmaid said she was very proper, nicely dressed, not the type of woman who usually comes there. 'A bit long in the tooth,' so the girl said, but still a handsome enough woman. So, even our staid old family retainer, Marshall, leads a hidden life!" Toby sounded very amused.

But I wasn't; this just added another link to the chain of mysteries at Octagon House, where nothing was as it seemed.

Chapter Fifteen

I tried to lift my head off the pillow, but it was too heavy. Struggling to open my eyes, I felt they were weighted with sand. With a tremendous effort I raised myself on my elbows and squinted at a room that swam.

What in the world was wrong with me? A kind of dull stupor fogged my brain. I couldn't think where I was or what time it was.

Cautiously I swung my legs over the side of the bed, steadied myself by gripping the edge of the mattress, and sat there for a moment, aware of a pounding head and an uneasy stomach. I gritted my teeth against a wave of nausea and wondered if I would feel better if I managed to get on my feet.

After a while the dizziness began to pass, and gradually my cobwebby mind cleared itself. I still had no idea what time of day it might be. The gray outside the windows gave no clue; it could be dawn or late afternoon. Shakily I reached for my lapel watch, which I had taken from my blouse the night before as usual and placed on my bedside table. It took a while for my bleary eyes to make out the tiny numerals and delicate hands. Incredibly it was twenty minutes past noon.

How could I have slept so long and so heavily? Every other night here at Octagon House, I'd lain sleepless for hours. Yesterday had been a day filled with one troubling incident after the other, and yet, unbelievably, I'd fallen asleep and evidently slept through the night without waking once.

My knees felt like aspic as I stood up. Holding on to the bedposts, I glanced in the mirror over the bureau. I looked ghastly — pale, heavy-eyed, my hair falling in a dark mass around my face and shoulders.

Was I coming down with something? Surely not. I was in perfect health yesterday, I reminded myself. What I needed was a good strong cup of coffee.

It took me an age to dress. Each garment seemed difficult to put on right, button, and hook. When I went to do up my hair, my brush felt like lead, and the hairpins kept falling out of my clumsy fingers as I wound the strands into a coil.

When at last I managed to look presentable, I went out the door and started down the hall to the stairway, still feeling light-headed. At the top of the steps I clutched the banister, feeling faint. It was then I heard loud, angry voices coming from the second floor, from Aunt Octavia's wing.

"Liar! That's right, you're a liar, Elvira, always have been."

I clung with both hands to the stair railing, paralyzed. So Elvira was having *her* interview with Aunt Octavia. From the sound of it things were going very badly.

"Ever since you were a child, you had sneaky ways. I recognized it in you then, but I thought I could correct it." Aunt Octavia made no effort to conceal her disdain. "Goodness knows, I tried. You were punished enough for lying when you lived here. I would have thought you might have outgrown it. But no! I could see the first evening listening to you that you hadn't.

"All that talk about your travels, your high life, the entertaining and being entertained, the name-dropping! Ha!" Aunt Octavia's voice was iced with sarcasm. "Did you think you were impressing me? Certainly not. I could see through your pretenses, as I have always been able to do.

"And you came here expecting something from me?" Her voice rose shrilly. "Well, *don't!* You couldn't possibly imagine I'd be so foolish as to choose a *liar* for the sole inheritor of this magnificent estate."

Then I heard Elvira's voice. Her voice, as loud as Aunt Octavia's had been, was filled with anger, frustration, and wounded pride. The rebellious child she had always been burst through the sophisticated veneer, and with a child's disregard for the consequences, Elvira seemed to have lost control. Her voice quivered with rage as she flung back furiously, "Of course I came back here expecting something. Why else would any of us come back here? We have as much right to this house, the Vale estate, as *you* do! But you're cruel and it pleases you to manipulate and pull strings and dangle rewards, spinning spiderlike traps and drawing us all into your web like poor flies. Well, two can play at this game, Aunt Octavia. You may see through me, but I see through *you* as well. You're a wicked old woman! You've alienated everyone. And you haven't heard the last of this despicable plan to cheat *me* and Toby out of what is rightfully ours!"

Horrified, I couldn't move. I stood there like a statue even as I heard the sound of running feet, the swish of taffeta skirts. Elvira came rushing up the stairs to the third floor steps, where I stood on the landing. Seeing me, she halted. Her face was crimson, contrasting cruelly with her flame-red hair, her expression distorted with fury.

"Well, Julie, of course you heard all that!" she said, her green eyes flashing. "What an insufferable despot that terrible old woman is! She delights in torturing. Well, I'm through dancing to her tune!" Elvira fixed me with a dagger-sharp gaze. "Since it's obviously *not* going to be Toby or me — then it must be *you!*" Her mouth twisted as she spoke. "So, Julie, how does it feel to be an heiress?"

"No, Elvira — no — wait —" I put out my hand to touch her arm, but she shook it off, hurrying to her room. I winced at the slam of the door. I didn't have a chance to tell her that I had made up my mind not to accept the position of sole inheritor even *if* it were offered, that I planned to tell Aunt Octavia so.

Now I saw Elvira was too upset to listen. I'd have to wait until she calmed down.

The downstairs part of the house was deserted. Toby was nowhere about. I went out to the kitchen, where to my surprise Lutie, her hat and coat on, was starting out the back door.

"Why, Miss Julie, I thought you was going to sleep all day!" she exclaimed.

"I don't know why I slept so soundly," I said. "Any chance of a cup of coffee?"

"Of course." She turned back to the stove and got down a cup and saucer from the shelf.

"I can wait on myself, Lutie, if you were going out."

"Well, I am, but I can take a few minutes. I'm glad to have the chance to tell you myself about supper. I told Toby to tell you, but you know him! Can't depend on him to carry a message." She chuckled.

She filled my cup. "He says the two of you was up till all hours," she commented. "My, oh, my, did he have a head on him this morning! Marshall says he finished a bottle of Miss Octavia's best brandy!" She raised an eyebrow at me. "Don't tell me you helped him with *that?*"

The brandy! It suddenly struck me that it might have been the brandy that made me so dense and disoriented this morning. But I'd barely had one glass! That shouldn't have had that much of an effect.

"Where is he now?"

"Went out a while ago. Didn't say where to or when he'd be back. I've fixed a cold supper for you three to help yourselves to this evening. Miss Octavia will have hers on a tray upstairs, and Mr. Victor's going out for dinner tonight, so it will be just the three of you. It'll be a nice chance for you to have a good chat by yourselves like old times, now, won't it?"

I wondered! With things as they stood, I doubted the three of us would have much to say to one another.

"I'm going to my nephew's wedding, so I won't be back until tomorrow afternoon. Miss Octavia give me permission some time ago, before it was known you three was coming for a visit," Lutie said. "Have you had a nice time together? You were always so companionable as children. Of course, Mr. Toby was always up to some mischief." She chuckled. "Remember the time he shut you up in the dumbwaiter?"

I had to laugh. I'd almost forgotten that time. We used to think it was great fun to use the dumbwaiter for our own elevator between the floors. Its original purpose was to bring baskets of laundry from upstairs down to the washroom off the kitchen and send clean sheets and towels back up to the bedroom floors. One day I'd climbed in, and Toby was to pull the ropes and bring me down, but instead he left me stranded midway and ran off in high glee. Lutie had been the one to hear my screams of terror and get me out.

"I'd forgotten that one," I said, but even as I laughed, I remembered another time, one that had been even worse — I'd been locked and left in the cupola.

"Well, I best be off," Lutie said, picking up her string bag and umbrella. "It looks as if we're in for some kind of storm, rain or snow," she declared. "Now, Marshall will put out what I prepared on the buffet in the dining room. There's cold chicken, two kinds of salad, scalloped potatoes to be heated in the chafing dish, and pie and walnut cake for dessert."

"Sounds wonderful, Lutie," I said. "Have a lovely time at the wedding."

After she left I poured myself another cup of coffee and sat at the kitchen table slowly sipping it. Gradually I began to feel better. Staring out the window, I tried mentally to rewrite my letter to Jordan. I saw that the rain had turned into snow and was falling fast, coating the windowsill.

The day stretched ahead of me, gray and quiet. With Elvira brooding in her room, Toby, only who knew where in Woodvale, Aunt Octavia secluded in her suite of rooms, the house was deadly still.

I left the kitchen and went back upstairs. I would write my note to Jordan and then maybe wander down to the small parlor and

168

look for a book to read to while away the rest of the afternoon. I hoped by evening both my cousins would be in a better frame of mind, and we could discuss our situation like rational adults.

To my astonishment, as I came up to the third floor, I saw Miss Ingersoll standing at my bedroom door. The door was ajar, and I could not tell whether she was coming out or going in. I felt a flicker of indignation that she was intruding on my privacy. I quickened my step, and as if alerted, she turned around. Her face reddened and for a moment she looked flustered. Then she gave her head a little toss, setting the starched wings of her nurse's cap aflutter, and said, "Oh, it's you, Miss Madison. I was looking for Miss Elvira's room. She has a migraine and asked me to bring her some headache powders." She put her hand in her apron pocket and brought out several small paper envelopes.

"Miss Elvira's room is across the hall," I said coolly. I had the feeling that the nurse *had* been in my room, and I resented it.

She walked briskly past me, and I watched her as she knocked on Elvira's door and waited. I heard something that sounded more like a moan than an answer, and Miss Ingersoll opened the door, slipped inside, and closed it.

I sat down at my desk and tried again to compose a note to Jordan.

"Dear Jordan, I wanted to say all this to you in person, but there may not be time. The longer I'm here, the more I realize it was a mistake to come."

I didn't get very far this time, either. Even with the two cups of coffee I'd had, my mind still felt muddled, and I found myself drowsy. After a few more unsuccessful attempts, I put down my pen, lay down on the bed, pulled the afghan around me, and went to sleep.

When I woke up, the room was full of shadows. I sat up with a jerk, realizing I must have slept away the afternoon. I got up quickly, poured water from the pitcher into the washbowl, and splashed my face. Hurriedly I redid my hair and went out of the bedroom into the hall.

I paused outside Elvira's door, but there was no sound. Miss Ingersoll's powders must have taken effect; Elvira must be sleeping off her migraine. I went past, down the steps, and found Toby in the drawing room, where a fire was crackling in the fireplace.

"Marshall says Elvira doesn't want to be disturbed, so it's just us for supper tonight, Julie." He smiled. "Actually, I'm glad. I've still got a lot of things I want to talk to you about."

Together we went into the dining room, where two places were set at the long table and candles were burning in the tall silver candelabra. We helped ourselves to Lutie's bountiful provisions. By now, not having eaten all day, I was ravenous.

We both ate hungrily and did not talk much. Our dinner plates empty, Toby cut us each a piece of walnut cake and brought it to the table. I poured us coffee.

"I've been thinking," he said. "Perhaps, Aunt Octavia will deal another hand. Who knows, maybe next time I may turn up the winning card." He gave a short, sardonic laugh, and his face hardened slightly. I had a sudden flash of insight. It was as unexpected as it was unwanted. I saw that behind Toby's charm was someone shrewd and calculating, someone I didn't know.

He poured cream into his coffee and said slowly, "Besides, I don't think she likes Elvira, even if she *is* the oldest and most logical one to pick, and I think —"

I never got to hear what Toby thought nor to tell him that Elvira had already had her session with our aunt, because just then Marshall came into the room and said, "Miss Julie, when you've finished your dinner, Miss Octavia would like you to come up to her room."

"Ah-hah, Julie. Now it's *your* turn before the Grand Inquisitor. Have you got any skeletons in the closet that she might unearth to put you out of the running, too?" Toby asked sarcastically.

Suddenly I wanted to put an end to all this speculation and make it clear once and for all that I was not eligible for this distasteful role in our aunt's scheme. But I thought that out of courtesy I should tell her first instead of discussing it any more with Toby. He and Elvira would learn soon enough that I wasn't in their way.

As I came up to the second-floor landing, I saw Marshall standing in the shadowy alcove in front of Aunt Octavia's sitting room, deep in conversation with Miss Ingersoll. At my approach they hastily broke apart, and Miss Ingersoll turned on her heel and disappeared into her own room, which adjoined my aunt's. Marshall, bearing a tray, nodded briefly as he passed me going down the stairs.

I took a long breath, braced myself, and knocked on Aunt Octavia's door.

Chapter Sixteen

Aunt Octavia was not in her sitting room when I entered, but I could hear movement in the adjoining bedroom, and she called to me from there, "I'll be with you presently, Julie."

I had not been in Aunt Octavia's wing of the house for years, so I took this opportunity to look around. The room appeared square but had wedges of alcoved window recesses which conformed to the outer octagon shape of the house.

The furniture was the heavy, mahogany kind of the period in vogue when the house was first built and furnished. There were only a few personal touches, mainly family pictures and portraits that filled one wall. I walked over to take a closer look.

There was one of Uncle Victor as a young cadet at the military academy he had attended, another of Grandfather Vale in a tweed hunting suit, rifle in hand, booted foot on the neck of a magnificent multiantlered deer he had felled. There was one of the second Mrs. Clement Vale as an exquisite bride, one of Aunt Octavia at about age twenty, I guessed, striking-looking in a riding habit, gracefully seated on a handsome horse.

But the picture that attracted my attention most was one of my mother, Clemmy, which I had never seen before. She was dressed, I supposed, for her debut into society, in a fantasy of a gown. Its ruffled neckline showed off her beautiful sloping shoulders, and she wore elbow-length white kid gloves and carried a bouquet of roses. Her features were delicate, her eyes luminous, her smile radiant. I felt a lump rise in my throat. Of course, I had always thought my mother pretty, but I had never seen her like this.

"You are quite like her, you know." A voice behind me spoke sharply, and I turned around. I had not noticed Aunt Octavia entering the room, and I could not know how long she had been observing me studying my mother's portrait.

The remark surprised me after the numerous times I had heard just the opposite comment from my aunt. I did not reply. I was too shocked at my aunt's appearance.

She seemed to have aged visibly since our first night at Octagon House. Although as perfectly groomed as ever, she seemed to have shriveled; her eyes, though bright, were sunken into the deep hollows around them. Above the drawn, wrinkled face her elaborately coiffed hair looked like a theatrical wig, its gingery color in contrast to the almost gray cast of her skin. She bore little resemblance to the erect, graceful young horsewoman of the picture I had just viewed.

She waved one heavily ringed, misshapen hand toward a chair opposite the kidney-shaped desk as she moved haltingly to seat herself behind it. She picked up a sheaf of papers, shuffled them, and said, "You must have some idea why I wanted to see you, Julie. My lawyer, Ross Holden, has discussed with me the changes I intend to make in my will. Although nothing has been definitely decided as yet or done legally, I think you know my reasons for wanting *one* person in charge of the Vale estate."

I opened my mouth to tell her my decision, but there was no chance, for she continued speaking.

"Your cousins may have told you that I have thoroughly investigated them and find them both woefully lacking in the qualities I am looking for in whoever will take over from me — and I've come to the conclusion that *you* are the only one who has enough brains and ability and *integrity* to carry out the management of this estate."

"Aunt Octavia —" I started to interrupt, but she held up her hand to stop me.

"You *must* take the responsibility, however you *think* you feel now. It is your duty as a Vale. There is no one else I can trust."

"Please, Aunt Octavia, listen to me. As soon as you first outlined this plan to us, I *knew* I couldn't accept it — *if* the position of sole inheritor *was* offered to me. I don't *want* it, Aunt Octavia. I don't want to remain here administering such a large estate. I have my own life, my own way to find. . . ."

Aunt Octavia stared me down, and I heard my voice trail away. Her mouth was an inverted U bracketed by deep lines of disapproval. "Enough, girl! I don't believe a word of it. How, at twenty-three, could you possibly be so firmly convinced you don't want the power, the wealth, the prestige that would come with such an inheritance? No one in her right mind would turn down an opportunity such as I am offering you — unless you hope to gain more by doing so."

Incensed by her accusation I indignantly half-rose from my chair. "Whether you believe it or not, Aunt Octavia, it is true. My father gave me two guidelines on how to live my life — to follow my conscience and to stand by my convictions."

"You'll find those principles difficult to hold on to in the real world," Aunt Octavia retorted sarcastically, her face twisting contemptuously. "Your mother was a dreamer, your father an idealistic, head-in-the-clouds professor! A *philosophy* professor at that. Muddle-headed, if you ask me."

Angry words sprang to my mind in defense of my parents. But noticing the ugly, purplish flush suffusing my aunt's face, the pulsing veins throbbing in her forehead, I remembered Jordan's warnings about the possibility of a stroke, and I bit them back.

Aunt Octavia continued, "I'm disappointed in you, Juliette. I thought that bringing you up here at Octagon House had put some steel in your spine, that you would not be easily influenced by your unrealistic father. Evidently I was mistaken." She paused, then said, "Listen to me carefully, my girl, before you issue any ultimatum about this chance of a lifetime. If you reconsider, I won't blame you for this temporary lapse of good sense. But if I have to rethink my plans, the fact that you made it necessary to do so will not bode well for you."

The implied threat in her words made me furious but even more determined to stand my ground. I got to my feet, saying simply, "I'm sorry, Aunt Octavia, both that I have disappointed you and that you think I'm ungrateful. But I can assure you I will not change my mind. Under the circumstances I think it best that I leave Octagon House as soon as possible." And without waiting for her reaction, I went quietly out of the room.

I went straight to Elvira's bedroom and knocked on the door. Leaning close to the crack, I said in a low but insistent tone, "Please, Elvira, let me in, we need to talk."

I waited for a long minute, then knocked again, whispering, "Elvira, we *must* talk, please open the door."

I heard the squeak of bedsprings, some shuffling movement. At the same time I heard the front door downstairs open and close and Uncle Victor's voice boom, "It's really coming down out there. Our first real snowstorm of the year." I heard Toby's voice in reply but could not distinguish the words. Both men's voices drifted away, and I assumed they had gone into the parlor.

Just then the latch on Elvira's door slipped back, and she held the door open a few inches, squinting out at me. She looked dreadful. Her hair, uncombed and matted, stood out in Medusa-like disarray around her narrow, deathly pale face. The bottle-green velvet robe she clutched loosely around her with one skinny freckled hand fell off one bony shoulder.

"What do you want?" she demanded hoarsely.

I saw that the pupils of her eyes were dilated, and she was having difficulty focusing. I was really concerned and asked, "How's your headache?"

"Horrendous," she said wearily, then frowned. "But you didn't come to talk about my health, I'm sure."

"Well, no, but of course, I'm very sorry about your headache —"

She gave a half-laugh. "Thank you. Now, what is the *real* reason you want to talk to me, Julie? To lord it over me after my humiliating scene with Aunt Octavia?"

"Oh, Elvira, you must know me better than that!" I protested. "You're wasting your anger on me anyway. I don't want the job of sole inheritor, and I've told Aunt Octavia so."

That seemed to momentarily stun her; she opened the door wider and motioned me inside.

"What good will that do?" she said. "Aunt Octavia has a way of getting what she wants. I think she had this whole thing planned before she even had us come." Elvira sank down on the bed, punched up the pillows, stuffed them behind her, and leaned back. "Maybe it's time to tell the truth. What have I got to lose *now?*" She pushed back her hair impatiently. "When I first got that letter from her, I thought it was the *miracle* I needed. I staked everything to come here, Julie. New wardrobe, new luggage, new *me!* It's all charged, of course. But it was so important to me — more important than you can imagine, Julie." She sighed dramatically. "Drew and I have been having the most dreadful time. I can't tell you what it costs to live on the scale we do. Just to keep up, even without lavish entertaining" — she gave a little shudder — "we just never have seemed to recover from the financial panic in the stock market a few years ago. I'm sure you were aware of all the bank failures — Drew had invested heavily in some speculative stocks and invested for his clients as well. We were literally on the edge and slipping fast. I had already thought of asking Aunt Octavia for help — not help exactly, because I always felt we *deserved* some of the Vale money — but I didn't think we'd get it until after the old witch died. Then her *invitation* came." Elvira snarled the word *invitation*. "I had a feeling something was up. I told Drew he could count on me if he'd risk outfitting me elegantly. So I came determined to kowtow if I had to — and I did. For all the good it did me!" Her mouth worked nervously. "I really don't know what we're going to do, Julie. I thought for sure she'd name *me* —"

"She still might, Elvira. I'm not going to accept."

Elvira looked at me suspiciously, then rubbed her hand across her forehead. "Julie, my head's pounding. I'm really not even thinking straight. I think I'll have to take another one of those awful powders Ingersoll gave me. So —" She put shaky hands up to both temples.

I took the hint and went to the door. "Try and get some more rest, Elvira. We can discuss this tomorrow."

"I was planning to leave tomorrow. I couldn't wait to be gone from this dark, gloomy old house — didn't care if I ever heard the words Vale or Octagon House again in my life. Then I got this blasted headache —"

"Wait and see what happens tomorrow," I urged her. "Things may be a great deal different. Aunt Octavia may have to change her mind."

I went out, shut the door softly, and started across the hall to my own bedroom when I heard someone quietly call my name. It was Toby, just coming up the stairs.

"Well, are you *the* 'heiress apparent'?" he quipped, sauntering toward me.

I didn't want to talk right in front of Elvira's door, so I beckoned him into my room. As quickly as possible I gave him a capsulated version of my conversation with Aunt Octavia.

He looked skeptical and shook his head. "That was crazy, Julie. You should have taken the job, then done what Elvira suggested. Gotten power of attorney then sold off some of the timberland and split it among the three of us. When you declined, Julie, you cut Elvira and me out of our chance for any share at all. Aunt Octavia made no secret of how she feels about the two of us."

I felt as if he'd struck me. I really had not given a thought to the plan Elvira had come up with. It was true, I *had* only thought of myself. I had not wanted to be trapped here at Octagon House as our aunt's financial lackey.

"I'm sorry, Toby," was all I could think of to say.

He shrugged indifferently and changed the subject. "I was talking to Uncle Victor just now — told him I was leaving on the early train tomorrow — and he says Aunt Octavia had everything decided before we came." He raised an eyebrow. "You must know she's had us all tracked down, followed by private investigators, don't you? I believe Elvira and I were always out of the running. She just got us here so you'd come."

"Oh, Toby, I don't think so —"

"*He* should know, shouldn't he? After all, he's her brother, known her all his life. He says she never does anything without plotting it out to the last minor detail. I don't think she's going to let you off the hook so easily, Julie."

He walked over to the door, saying, "By the way, Uncle Victor's all excited about something; he was going up to talk to Aunt Octavia. I left him on the second floor as I came up here."

I followed him to the door as he opened it. "I hope you're wrong, Toby. I wish Aunt Octavia would —"

I never got to finish saying what I wished our aunt would do because as Toby and I stood there at my open door, we heard a furious argument taking place just below us. We exchanged a startled glance. It was Uncle Victor's voice uncharacteristically raised. Uncle Victor, always the soul of gentility, courtesy, and good manners — shouting?

"We'll just see about this, Octavia. I'll talk to a lawyer — *tomorrow!* There must be a way I can have access to the trust fund Father left me. We'll see who has the last word on this!"

Uncle Victor must have started to walk away, and Aunt Octavia must have hobbled to her door to call after him, because her voice rang out so sharp and clear we heard every syllable.

"You always were a fool, Victor. Father thought so, too! Why else would he have passed over his son and put me in charge of the estate? Getting married at your age! Well, there's no fool like an old fool, they say, and that's true in your case. And to a namby-pamby old spinster like Martha MacAndrews; you surely are out of your mind!"

Evidently Uncle Victor declined to retort; we heard his door shut firmly, and then total silence descended. Toby and I continued to stare at each other wordlessly. Then, with a shrug and a little salute, Toby turned and, hands in his pockets, went down the corridor to his own room.

Horror upon horror in this hate-filled

house, I thought, discovering I was trembling. Back inside my room I went over to the window, rested my hot cheek against the frosty pane. Looking out into the dark night, I saw steadily falling snow. Drifts were piling up along the driveway.

How could Jordan and I ever find our way back to each other surrounded by all this maliciousness and Aunt Octavia's perverse mischief? I would have to go away from here, out from under the malignant influence of Octagon House and all its pervasive unhappiness. I could go back to the town where I'd lived with my father, get another position at the college. If Jordan was serious about renewing our romance, he could come there. Perhaps, there, away from all this, we could find each other again.

I must try to make Jordan understand my feelings. I sat down at the little desk and tried again to write to him.

"It is certain now that Aunt Octavia has named me as the sole inheritor of the Vale fortune. She told me so today. She wants me to stay here, giving me a generous allowance, while she teaches me about investments, stocks, and bonds and I consult with lawyers, attend board meetings, and learn how to manage the estate."

I paused, pen poised above the sheet of

paper. I thought of Toby and Elvira, how disappointed they were, how fearful that now they would be cut entirely out of the will. Had I been selfish in turning down our aunt's offer?

It was too late, I was too tired to think. I would try to get some sleep, and tomorrow — tomorrow?

For some reason the Biblical admonition flashed into my mind: "Sufficient for the day is the evil thereof...." A second thought followed fast: "This is an *evil* house." I didn't know where *that* came from, but it was almost as if it had been spoken out loud.

I shivered. I put down my pen and went to bed feeling discouraged and depressed.

Chapter Seventeen

When I woke up, my bedroom was filled with an unusual, glaring brightness. A glance at my watch told me it was still quite early, so I got up and went to the window. Snow was still falling and the lawn was already blanketed; the spruce trees lining the driveway were frosted pyramids, and the pedestaled iron deer in its circled center was heavily coated white.

I dressed and went by Elvira's still-closed door. Toby's bedroom door was ajar, but there was no sign of him. The second floor was silent, and when I went on downstairs, I found that no one was in the front part of the house, either. I walked back to the kitchen. There I found Toby scrambling some eggs for himself. He looked up and grinned as I came in.

"Looks as though we're going to have to avail ourselves of our aunt's hospitality a little longer. There's already a good three feet of snow fallen, and it doesn't look as though it's ready to stop. Nothing's moving down on the road as far as I could see from my window. I think this is a good old-fashioned blizzard, Julie." He laughed. "What fun! To be snowbound at Octagon House."

"Lutie isn't here?" I looked around. Toby, busy stirring, did not answer, but I could have guessed his answer from the spilled milk, the scattered eggshells, and the number of pots and pans about on counters.

"I don't think anyone could get through with the roads like this. She's probably snowed in, too, over at her sister's," Toby commented, then held up the skillet and asked, "Want some? There's plenty."

"No, thanks, but is there any coffee?"

"Made a whole pot. Is Elvira coming down?"

"Think she's still asleep. Trying to get rid of a monstrous headache."

Toby seated himself at the table and began to eat; I brought my coffee over and sat down opposite him.

"After I finish, I'm going to go out and see how deep it is, then try to get down to the road, at least, and see what's happening."

"Not much from the looks of things," I said dismally, realizing that even if I'd been ready to leave Octagon House today, there was no way I could go.

The rest of the day passed slowly. The snow continued and Octagon House seemed wrapped in a dense, white cloak. Everything seemed muted, even the striking of the clock in the downstairs hall.

Elvira never emerged from her room all day. Uncle Victor, closeted in his wing of the house, only appeared briefly, looking distracted and preoccupied. Miss Ingersoll said Aunt Octavia was not feeling well and would remain in bed. Toby had disappeared after breakfast, and I couldn't help wondering if somehow he had managed to make it into Woodvale to the tavern.

I found a Jane Austen novel I had not read in years in the parlor bookcase and curled up with it in my room. Every once in awhile I'd get up and look out the window to mark the progress of the snowstorm.

I tried rewriting my letter to Jordan a couple of times, but these attempts ended like the others; discarded. I couldn't seem to find the right words to say everything that was in my mind and heart.

Marshall had shoveled his way over from his place above the carriage barn and later came to tell me he had set out a cold roast, a loaf of bread, some butter and jam, and applesauce for a buffet supper.

I went into Elvira's darkened room and asked if I could bring her up something to eat. She moaned that her stomach was upset, but she would try some tea.

I fixed it and took it up to her, then joined Uncle Victor and Toby in the dining room.

Hearing that Elvira was confined to bed fighting a migraine, Uncle Victor remarked apologetically, "I'm afraid this has not been a very happy homecoming for you three." With a sad shake of his head, he added, "But then, this is not a happy house. Actually, it's never been as far back as I can remember."

We all retired to our rooms early, and it was still snowing when I got ready to go to bed.

The next day was much the same, although it stopped snowing. The house remained strangely silent. Late in the afternoon Elvira reappeared, looking wan but better. Later still, to my surprise, I heard Jordan's voice in the hall downstairs.

I jumped off the bed, ran my brush quickly through my hair to smooth it, and after a hurried glance in the mirror rushed out into the hall. I leaned over the third floor banister in time to see Jordan, accompanied by Miss Ingersoll, coming up the stairway.

I gathered he had come to check on Aunt Octavia. He proceeded down the hall toward her wing without looking up. But much to my chagrin someone else had observed me eagerly bending over the balcony to watch him. As I turned around, I saw Elvira, a cunning smile on her face.

Looking like a cat who had just polished off a dish of cream, she said archly, "He *is* quite handsome, isn't he? Half the girls at school were mad about him, I remember. Were you one of them?" Elvira's eyes narrowed, glinting maliciously. I felt myself blush under that gaze.

"Oh, I don't know —" I stammered.

"Don't be so coy, Julie," she teased. "There's nothing wrong with fanning old flames as long as you're here. After all, he *is* Aunt Octavia's physician, so it might be to your advantage to cultivate him again. Let's go down and waylay him when he finishes with her and ask him to stay for a sherry."

Before I could object, she had slipped her hand through my arm in girlish companionship and was leading me down the steps. I didn't want to make a fuss and draw even more attention to the fact that I was interested in Jordan, so I went along.

We found Toby alone in the parlor. Glad of company, he rose and played host with the decanter of sherry. When we heard footsteps on the stairway, Elvira immediately went to the door that led into the hall and cordially invited Jordan to join us.

As he came in he glanced over at me, but suddenly shy I looked down into my glass. Why did I feel so awkward and tongue-tied? Was it the thought of that kiss, which had stirred me so deeply and brought back all the remembered pulsing desire for him, that now caused me embarrassment? Maybe, because I was afraid I'd give myself away under Elvira's scrutiny.

However, Jordan seemed perfectly comfortable. Accepting the sherry from Toby, he talked to my cousins easily. He told us that Woodvale had experienced a full-blown blizzard, the first in twenty years. Trains were not running, since the tracks were blocked, and only a few hardy souls were moving about on foot or in sleighs.

"Luckily, Uncle Hugh was used to this kind of winter after practicing here for over forty years and kept a one-horse sleigh. I was able to get it out early this morning. I had patients I needed to see, and, of course, your aunt was one of them."

Elvira was solicitous at once. "How is dear Aunt Octavia?" she asked, her face a picture of concern.

"Not well, I'm afraid. As I mentioned to Julie" — he looked at me intently, and I felt color rise hotly into my cheeks — "all the excitement connected with your visit here has not been good for her, I'm sorry to say. Her blood pressure is way up, always a concern. Your aunt has had a series of small strokes. Nothing serious — as yet — still, we don't like patients with her history to exert themselves or get too excited. I ordered her to stay in bed and directed Miss Ingersoll to see that she obeys." He smiled slightly. "Your aunt can be quite a difficult patient. Very stubborn." Again he glanced at me. "I think it must run in the family."

Elvira laughed, a high, tinkly, affected laugh. "I know what you mean! I'm afraid it *is* in the Vale blood."

She had not missed Jordan's eyes resting on me, and a minute later she got to her feet and with a meaningful glance at Toby said, "I must go see Marshall about dinner. Toby, would you check on the wine? Jordan — I can't yet bring myself to call you *Dr. Barret!* — Would you stay and dine with us? Our cook is stranded somewhere and it will be pot-luck, I'm afraid. But we'd all be delighted if you would; am I right, Julie?"

I could have strangled her. Jordan, however, handled the invitation coolly. "Thank you, Elvira, but I have to get over to the hospital. I wasn't able to get out yesterday, and I have patients to attend to. But thank you."

"Another time, perhaps, while we are *all* still here!" she said flirtatiously. "It would be like old times."

Since Elvira had been ill with flu at the beginning of our romance and had left Octagon House to live with her mother and stepfather the following summer, I didn't know to what "old times" she referred. I could see Jordan's amusement as she gave a coquettish little wave and, with Toby in tow, left the room.

"Extraordinary!" he murmured after they went out. I wasn't sure what he meant. Then he set down his sherry glass and came slowly toward me. I stood quite still as if mesmerized. We were inches apart now, and he whispered "extraordinary" again.

I don't know which of us moved first, but all at once I was in his arms, my face lifted to his kiss. It was a deep and compelling kiss, and I realized it was the kiss I had longed for every time I thought of Jordan.

Then, aware that someone might walk in at any moment, I pulled back out of his arms, but I couldn't look away from his eyes. I felt breathless and strangely frightened. I wasn't sure why. Then, without thinking, I blurted out, "Oh, Jordan, Aunt Octavia's designated *me* to be the sole inheritor."

194

I saw his expression change. His eyes widened, something curious flickered in their depths, and a kind of subtle alteration took place.

"Just that? She hasn't changed any of the provisions, has she?" His voice was sharp, intense. "Everything will remain the same, won't it? She hasn't had Ross Holden make any *legal* changes, has she? It will only mean that you will administer the estate, right?"

"I don't know, I didn't —" I began.

A strange expression passed over Jordan's face, his eyes narrowed speculatively. He stepped back from me, frowning, and said thoughtfully, "Well, *that* should be all right, as long as she made no changes — *that* was what concerned me." Then, almost as if he were talking to himself, Jordan continued, "She promised Uncle Hugh, reassured him over and over, and of course, she repeated that assurance to me. Surely she wouldn't have changed her mind. . . ."

I felt a sudden chill. Why was Jordan so interested in Aunt Octavia's will? With a strange fascination I noticed the set of Jordan's jaw, the intensity of his expression as he spoke.

For some reason Jordan had been worried that Aunt Octavia was going to change her will. Was it because that would endanger some bequest he had been counting on? I remembered what the housekeeper, Mrs. Hammond, had said about both Jordan and his uncle jumping to Aunt Octavia's commands. When the three of us arrived, and there was uncertainty about which one of us would be named executrix, had Jordan feared a change of the will would mean a change of fortune for him?

Had the possible loss of some promised legacy influenced Jordan's interest in me? I remembered our first hostile meeting, and then how he had tried later to reestablish our relationship. Was it because he thought I would become sole inheritor, with the power to administer bequests?

The melting warmth I still felt after his touch, his kiss, the surging of awakened desire, all drained away.

I looked at Jordan and slowly my fragile dreams shattered as might the delicate wineglass I held; my hope of regaining the love I had once lost now faded. Was Jordan vying for wealth just like Toby and Elvira? The country doctor expecting to be rewarded for his attention to a difficult but immensely rich old patient?

Suspicion is an insidious thing; once planted, it grows quickly, replacing any other emotion.

My whole body stiffened. I could feel an icy shell enclosing the softness of my heart. I don't know what I would have said or done if at that very moment Uncle Victor had not entered the room and greeted Jordan jovially. During their exchange of trivialities, I managed to murmur an excuse and slip out of the room.

I went directly upstairs to my room, and I did not return to bid Jordan good night. I stood rigidly at the window in my unlighted bedroom, and after a while I watched Jordan's horse and sleigh glide down the driveway and out of sight.

Chapter Eighteen

Elvira flung down her cards and exclaimed, "If I have to spend another day like this, I shall go mad!"

Elvira and I were sitting in the parlor, where, at her insistence, I had agreed to play double solitaire. This was our third game. It had stopped snowing, but the roads were uncleared, the trains were not running yet, and we were still snowbound.

Toby came in while we were playing and moved restlessly from window to fireplace and back to the window. Finally he turned around and said, "Listen, you two, I have a wonderful idea. That is, if you're game. I've just been outside, and there's a great icy crust on the snow, perfect for sledding. We could bundle up and go to the top of Hemlock Hill, and sled like we used to when we were kids!"

"On what?" I asked, eager for any change but unsure if this plan was it.

"Our old wooden sleds. They must be

around here someplace. Aunt Octavia never throws anything out."

His enthusiasm was catching. "That *would* be a lark!" I agreed, putting down my card hand with relief and getting up. Getting out of the house into the clear fresh air would be a welcome change from this boring card game I'd been coerced into.

"You're both out of your minds," jeered Elvira.

"Don't be a spoilsport, Elvira," retorted Toby. "You don't want to remain a prisoner in here. You're not so old that you can't see the fun of it, are you? It's not that cold. The sun is bright, and once we get to the top of the hill, we'll be warm in no time. Come on, Elvira," he urged. "Where's your sense of adventure?"

I was glad to see that the world-weary look on Toby's face had vanished like magic his eyes shining with anticipation. Toby was a boy again.

"Look," he said, "the sleds are probably up in the attic or out in the woodshed. I'll go round up Marshall and get him to help me find them." With that he bounded out of the room in search of Marshall.

"Why do you encourage him in this non-sense?" asked Elvira querulously, stacking the cards again. "Really, Julie, you are both demented."

"Oh, come on, Elvira," I coaxed. "All you've done is complain about how dull it is around here. Now here's a chance to do something impetuous and fun. *You* used to be the one who came up with all the ideas for our good times and Toby and I followed like sheep."

"Oh, all right, if you must put it that way." She sighed. "But it truly *is* ridiculous, you know, three grown people going sledding like children. I doubt if I have anything warm enough to wear."

"I'm sure between us we can find something. Let's go see," I suggested, starting out of the room. Still murmuring small objections, Elvira followed.

We were at the second-floor landing when we saw Miss Ingersoll backing out of Aunt Octavia's room carrying a tray. Our aunt's strident voice echoed into the hall. We heard Miss Ingersoll's usually crisp professional tone change into a whining injured one. I felt Elvira's talon-sharp fingers clutch my arm, halting me.

"I don't have to take this kind of abuse, Miss Vale. I'm a qualified nurse, and I can leave at any time. Hospitals are crying for good nurses. Why, I turned down a *supervi-*

sor's position at a Boston hospital to stay here and care for your stepmother. *She* promised me that if I did, I'd be well rewarded for all my years of devotion —"

"Oh, get out of here, Ingersoll!" Aunt Octavia cut her off. "Nobody's making you stay, so don't talk to me about *wasted* years! You've been paid well, *very* well, I'd say. So if you're not satisfied, then leave! What's stopping you? Too old to get another job?" Her tone harshened. "Don't expect a reference from me if you decide to leave. Not after this display of impudence. How would you explain the last twenty years, eh? What would a prospective employer assume if you could not account for *twenty* years?" Aunt Octavia's voice turned vicious. "Maybe they'd think you'd been in prison or an insane asylum, eh? I'd advise you to be careful the next time you start to complain to me about what you think is *owed* you."

The door was pulled shut, preventing Aunt Octavia from giving further threats, and Miss Ingersoll came bustling along the corridor toward the stairway.

Then she saw us and stopped short. Realizing we must have overheard the ugly exchange, her face turned beet-red, contorted with rage and humiliation. Caught in the act of eavesdropping, we stared back at her in stricken horror. Trying to control her fury, she managed to say, "Your aunt is having a bad day. It's not unusual with patients in her condition. Most of the time I don't let it bother me, but sometimes I do lose patience. I think it's not being able to get out for my daily constitutional because of the snow."

I almost felt sorry for her as she struggled to contain her anger.

Then taking on a self-pitying tone, she said, "But, then, what would you two know of *my* kind of day-to-day devotion, year in year out with hardly a word of thanks . . ." Her mouth tightened into a grim line. Her head went up; and not glancing at us again, she moved swiftly downstairs.

Elvira raised her eyebrows. "Well, now, Aunt Octavia has managed to alienate *everyone* in this house!" she declared. "She'd be in a fine fix if Ingersoll *did* leave — if all of us just walked out —"

"Except Marshall," I reminded her, half-joking.

"Oh, yes, Marshall! The indestructible, unflappable Marshall," she said sarcastically. "Maybe that's just because he knows where all the family skeletons are buried!"

"Oh, Elvira you're incorrigible!" I laughed and we went the rest of the way up the stairs together.

While I got together as warm an assortment of clothes as I could find, I could not help thinking about Ingersoll. Was she worried that Aunt Octavia's designated "sole inheritor" would cut *her* promised legacy from Grandmother Vale out of the will?

Was that the reason I sometimes caught her looking at me or Toby or Elvira with undisguised dislike? Did she see us as a threat to her long-hoped-for security?

"Hurry up, Julie!" Toby called outside my bedroom door. "Marshall and I found the sleds. We're taking them down to clean and wax the runners now. It'll take us awhile to walk through the woods up to Hemlock Hill, and these winter afternoons are short. So hurry."

Toby was waiting with the sleds when we came out on the back porch. At the last minute Elvira put up a fuss. "I'm not sure I want to go. It looks like it's clouding up, and it's probably getting colder."

"Come on, Elvira," I encouraged her. "Once we're walking you'll be warm enough."

"You can't back out now, Elvira, we're all set," Toby said firmly. "Here's your sled, and this one's Julie's," he said, handing me the rope to pull it with.

Miss Ingersoll, bundled to her ears, came

out as we were setting off. "My, my!" she clucked her tongue. "Off for some winter sport, eh?"

Elvira did not answer, and I just nodded. We were both still embarrassed at having been witness to the nurse's humiliating scene with Aunt Octavia. Toby, however, smiled broadly and asked, "Want to come along? We can take turns on the sleds."

"No, thank you. A brisk walk is all I need. Besides, I can't be away from my patient too long," Miss Ingersoll replied.

She was still standing on the porch watching us as we started off, dragging our sleds in the direction of Hemlock Hill. The air was clear and invigorating. Our boots made a satisfying sound as they broke into the new snow. Soon even Elvira began to enjoy herself as we crunched along, laughing and chattering like children. The years seemed to roll away and with them some of the recent tension and guardedness that had developed between us since Aunt Octavia's pronouncement. Somehow the three of us seemed to recapture our old camaraderie.

Temporarily, I tried to put aside my suspicion about Jordan. How could I have been so wrong about him? Was there no one I could trust?

But I refused to let my troubling thoughts spoil this outing. Anyway, as soon as possible I planned to get the first train out and leave Woodvale forever. I didn't care what happened to the Vale fortune.

We trudged along single-file with Toby leading the way, Elvira next and me at the end. Because the snow was deeper than we realized, each step took all our energy and after the first few minutes we stopped talking to one another.

I was soon panting with the effort. For the past few years the easy walk from our home over to the college campus was about the extent of my exercise. Gradually my steps slowed and the other two got further ahead of me and I had to halt to catch my breath.

It was then I had the uneasy feeling we were being followed. I half turned to look behind me, thinking I heard something. A gust of wind knocked a clump of snow from the branch of a tall pine tree and I realized the movement of the sweeping bough and its shadow on the snow was what I had imagined was the figure of a person.

Toby reached the top of the hill first. He waved both hands, shouting triumphantly.

"Come on, slow pokes! Wait until you see the view, it'll be worth it."

"It better be!" Elvira yelled back. Turning

back to me, she called, "I don't know why I let you two talk me into this."

I for one agreed with Toby when I reached the crest of the hill. The valley below looked like a Christmas card. Woodvale — its houses, churches, barns, and other buildings topped with dollops of snow — looked like a toy village against the cloudless blue sky. Behind us were the woods we had come through, deep and dark and green. The snow on the hill was pristine, untrodden.

"We'll have to make our own tracks," Toby stated. "We'll each have to take a few runs, then gradually the snow will get packed down and slicker, and give us a better slide."

Taking his suggestion we each began a separate path from which to launch our sleds, a good six feet apart from one another. Toby challenged the steepest part of the hill out of our sight, Elvira took a more gently sloping section, and I tackled a middle route. It was slow going.

In spite of the hard work of creating a sled track, we soon got into the fun of it. We trudged back up to the top again and again, enjoying the glide down more each time as it became smoother and faster.

We began to feel as carefree as children. Everything was forgotten in the wonderful freedom of the experience. Laughter and shouts rang out in the crystal air as we called to one another on the way up or down. All the gloom, depression, and troubled atmosphere at Octagon House faded in the glorious exhilaration of the present.

After a few runs I started having trouble with my rudder. It had loosened considerably since my first ride, and the sled tended to veer slightly off course as I went down. To control it better I changed to sledding boy-style like Toby, on my stomach, guiding it with my hands instead of my feet. I was having too much fun to consider whether it was lady-like. No one was going to see me, anyhow.

Skimming over the snow on the curving path down the hillside, taking the heart-stopping leap over two big hillocks, racing down an almost perpendicular trail was a breathtaking thrill . . . I lost track of the time rushing by. It had been so long since I'd had such pure pleasure; I felt intoxicated with the simple joy of it.

As I came up to the top again after one glorious ride, Toby motioned me over to his side of the hill.

"Try my track this time, Julie!" he urged.

"All right," I said, but Elvira interrupted.

"Look, you two, I think we should start back to the house." She stomped her feet and hugged her arms. "I'm getting cold, I've had enough. I think we should quit. It's a long way back to Octagon House remember."

"Not until Julie takes a turn on my track. It's great now, really slick, a thriller. Come on, Elvira, you should try it, too."

Elvira frowned. "No, Toby, I told you, I'm tired. Anyway, it will be dark soon." She shivered and pointed to the sky. "Look at the sun."

The winter sky was changing, the sun lower, the trees on the hills casting long purple shadows on the snow. But tempted by Toby's hint of another more exciting ride, I hated to give up.

"Let's, Elvira!" I begged.

"Oh, you two!" she said irritably. "If you want to, Julie, go ahead. I'm starting back."

"Spoil sport!" scoffed Toby. Glancing up from examining his sled runners, he gave Elvira a disgusted look.

The familiar tug of wills between my cousins began in the same pattern I'd become used to over the years. Ignoring them I pulled my sled over to Toby's track. Their voices continued as I set down my sled, pausing to pull the wool cap over my ears and adjust my mittens.

"Grow up, you two!" I shouted over my

shoulder in a vain attempt to stop the silly argument. Then as I bent down ready to mount my sled, out of the corner of my eye, I was aware of something moving behind me. It flashed through my mind that it was Toby ready to play some boyish prank and the words "Don't Toby!" formed on my lips. But before I could speak, a fierce shove on my back thrust me forward onto my sled, then an equally strong push sent my sled flying forward.

I barely had time to grab the rudder with my hands as I tried to position myself more securely. But I was already sweeping downhill at a terrifying rate because my runners had not had a chance to get set firmly into the track.

Faster and faster I sped. I was aware of another sled behind me, too close, but since it was all I could do to try and guide my own, I didn't dare look back to see who it was.

Steering soon became impossible. Suddenly my sled veered to one side, completely off the track, rushing at an incredible speed over the icy surface, heading right into a dark cluster of trees at the edge of the hill.

It all happened too fast for me to panic, even though some part of my consciousness knew I was plunging toward disaster. The front runners hit a rock, the sled nose-dived, my hands lost their grip on the rudder, and I toppled off the sled just before it flew off the cliff in front of me.

Desperately I clutched at a low branch of one of the pine trees at the edge, a clump of snow from its laden bough showering my face and temporarily blinding me. I clung to the branch for dear life, even as the scratchy needles clawed my face, my legs dangling over the drop.

My gasping breath was an aborted scream because instinctively I knew I was hanging precariously above the abandoned stone quarry at the bottom of Hemlock Hill.

My weight on the tree branch brought another avalanche of snow down upon me. I felt snow in my mouth; I blinked my eyes, trying to clear my vision. I was afraid to look down, realizing that I hung over a yawning gulch. My heart was banging and my breath was shallow, my legs flailing to find some foothold. I knew that somehow I had to pull myself back up, depending on the tree branch not to break under my weight until I could regain some ground.

Hand over hand I inched up the bough until, thankfully, one of my feet struck something solid. With tremendous effort I climbed back onto the edge of the cliff, never loosening my grip on the branch.

Trembling from the physical exertion and shivering from fright, I got to my knees and looked around, then slumped against the trunk of the rescuing tree. I chanced a look over the jutting promontory and far below saw my sled broken to bits in the chasm of the quarry.

A cold sweat drenched me as I realized had I not been thrown off the sled and been able to grab the tree branch, I would have plunged to my death on the rocks below. I felt sick. I closed my eyes, dizzy with my near escape from a fatal accident.

Too shaken to stand, I scooted slowly back from the terrifying overhang. My heart pounded as I painfully reached a safe distance from the gaping gorge. Then, panting, I struggled to my feet, my boots sinking deeply into the drifted snow.

Stunned, I looked around, straining to see if Toby or Elvira had seen what had happened and were coming to help me. But I saw no one. The hillside was deserted, and long shadows were now falling on the glistening snow. How far off the track had I skimmed? Should I try to climb back up to the top of the hill?

With no one in sight, I knew I had better get started because it was getting colder, and the sky was already darkening. The snow where I had landed was deep, and it took all my shaken strength to lift one foot at a time to make my way back up the hill.

The rising wind blew stinging pellets of loose snow in my face. I was shivering from nerves as well as the increasing cold. My boots were not made for snow hiking, and the leather was now wet; my feet and toes were freezing.

Clutching for support at the branches of the pines studding the hill I went step by step up the steep hillside in the deep, untrampled snow. Although the wind was penetratingly cold, I was perspiring from the laborious climb, panting with the effort, forced to stop to take long breaths. Surely Elvira and Toby had missed me and would be looking for me, and would have heard my cry for help. Should I try shouting?

I hardly had the strength to do so. It was so cold it was painful even to draw air into my lungs. Suddenly I stopped walking, trying to get my bearings. Had my fall off the sled turned me around so that I was climbing up the other side of the hill, not toward the spot we had started sledding? Where were Elvira and Toby? I tried to call, but my voice was quickly lost in the empty air.

Panic stirred in my stomach. I must not

go to pieces, I told myself. I must stay calm and figure out the best way up the hill. Once I reached the place where we had sledded, I could find the woods, and from there I could certainly find my way back to Octagon House.

But instead, the hillside seemed to grow steeper and the day darker. Soon there would be no light, and I would really be lost. I remembered that on the bottom of one side of the hill there was a stream cutting through the woods, and over it a bridge that led to the road into town. Maybe that would be the closest, safest way to try to get off the hill.

I stood still and strained to hear some sound. Gratefully, in the dense silence surrounding me, I heard the faint rush of water. Going sideways I slipped and slid down toward it. The water rushed by at a dizzying speed. Lightheaded still from the accident, I stopped and put my hand up to my head and felt a swelling mound. I must have hit my head on a stone under the snow when I was flung off the sled. I stood still for another minute, trying to locate the bridge. I could hear the rustle of the wind in the tree branches, the gush of the stream flow, the crackling of the ice crust of the snow under my boots. A horrible aloneness gripped me, a sense of isolation and fear. Where were my cousins? Why hadn't they come looking for me? Surely one of them had seen what happened? I thought another sled had followed me when I took off — then I remembered that powerful shove.

Had someone purposely sent me spinning over the icy snow, knowing that I could be hurtled to my death in the old stone quarry? Someone? One of my cousins?

A terrible realization gripped me. They both still thought I would be Aunt Octavia's choice as sole inheritor. Neither of them believed my assertion that I would not accept. Could it be that in their desperate need or greed one of them might have thought that with *one* potential heir gone, his or her own chances improved?

I stood there motionless, horrified.

Suddenly a branch behind me snapped and fell under its burden of snow. I jumped then another sound came: the crunch of booted footsteps breaking through the freezing snow? Was someone following me? Perhaps someone had been watching me from the shadows of the trees, had seen that I had not plunged to my death as they had planned — and now were going to see I died some other "accidental" way!

My frenzied imagination sent a scream

rushing to my throat. It became only a terrified gasp. I started to run, plunging through the snow, stumbling, staggering. I looked back over my shoulder and thought I saw a large dark figure gaining on me. Terror thrust me forward, and then I tripped over something, a stone concealed by the snow, and I fell, twisting my foot.

A blaze of crippling pain seared through me. For a moment I couldn't breathe or move. But spurred by my fear, I somehow managed to wrest myself out of the snow into which I had fallen, and, dragging my injured foot, I blundered on. The day's light was nearly gone when at last I saw the outline of the bridge, and sobbing, panting, I finally reached it.

Clinging to the railing, with my last ounce of strength, I pulled myself along until I reached the road. My ankle throbbed against my soggy boot, but I knew if I stopped, I'd never be able to go on. I did not even try to figure how many miles I was from Woodvale. In the distance I could see the lights of houses, and with desperation fueling my half-frozen body, I propelled myself through the darkness toward the nearest one.

Some instinct for survival carried me the rest of the way. I pushed through a gate, up shallow steps onto a porch, where a reassuring glow shone through the fanlight above the front door. I leaned, exhausted, against the door and pounded on it with numbed fists. Near collapse I prayed someone would come soon, that safety and warmth were only a few steps away. Then I heard approaching footsteps, and the door was flung open. My knees buckled and I fell into the arms of the tall man who had answered my knocking. Through the dizziness about to overtake me, I heard a voice.

"Julie! Julie! My God, what's happened?"

But I was beyond giving an explanation. I felt myself lifted up in strong arms. Before I lost consciousness I murmured his name: "Jordan —"

Chapter Nineteen

"Mrs. Hammond!" I heard Jordan call. "Bring blankets — and get some hot water boiling! At once!"

I couldn't seem to stop shivering. Jordan carried me over to the sofa and immediately pulled off my soaked boots. After ripping off my damp stockings, he began to rub my bare feet vigorously, but when he touched my injured ankle, I let out a cry of pain. He stopped at once, then pulled a knitted afghan from the end of the sofa and threw it over me, shouting again over his shoulder, "Hurry, Mrs. Hammond." To me he demanded, "Where have you been? What happened?"

I shook my head and tried to speak, but my teeth were chattering too much to answer. "Never mind," he said fiercely as he started unwinding the scarf still hanging limply around my head and throat. I made a feeble attempt to push back the wet strands of hair plastered against my cheeks and forehead. Then Jordan took my face in both hands and examined the scratches from the pine needles and the egg-sized bump on my brow.

When Mrs. Hammond hurried into the room, her arms laden with blankets, he directed, "Get these wet clothes off her, Mrs. Hammond, while I get some brandy." Then he strode out of the room.

"Oh, my poor dearie," his housekeeper murmured as she helped me out of my soaked jacket. "Let's get you up so's I can pull off this wet skirt." With her support I managed to stand as she unbuttoned my sweater and blouse. Down to my chemise and petticoat I was shuddering with a chill. The room began to swim. I swayed and said weakly, "I think I'm going to faint."

The next thing I knew I was lying in bed, wrapped in the comforting luxury of a down quilt, one foot resting on a flannel-encased hot-water bottle, the other bandaged and elevated on a pillow. Crackling logs burned cheerfully in the brick fireplace of the softly lighted room.

Jordan was sitting beside me, gently chafing my cold hands, a concerned expression on his face, his eyes more angry than anxious. I swallowed and discovered that my throat was very sore. I ran my tongue across dry lips and tried to say something, but he stopped me.

"Don't try to talk now, Julie," he said almost sternly. "Here's something to get your blood circulating again." He took a steaming mug from the table beside the bed, placed it into my hands, cupping his own over mine, and raised it to my mouth.

My first sip of the brandy-laced milk made me sputter as it went down my parched throat. But within seconds it seemed to permeate my body with a welcome warmth. My ordeal had made me achingly weary, and my eyelids began to droop. I struggled to fight the drowsiness, saying, "I should go —"

"Nonsense," Jordan retorted. "You're staying here tonight. I've already sent word up to Octagon House that you're safe, although it doesn't seem anyone was unduly alarmed about you." His words were sandpaper-rough with sarcasm.

"But —" I protested, "I can't —"

"Of course you *can* and you *are*. That's doctor's orders. Be sensible, Julie," Jordan said. "You're suffering from shock and exposure. You've a badly sprained ankle. You'll be lucky if you don't develop a case of pneumonia." A slight smile tugged at his lips. "Don't worry, you're well chaperoned.

Mrs. Hammond has settled you in the downstairs guest room, and she'll be back to sit with you." Eyes twinkling a little, he added, "Guarding you in case I should take advantage of the situation and make any improper advances."

I was too exhausted to blush and closed my eyes in spite of trying to keep them open.

When I opened them again, Mrs. Hammond was pushing aside chintz curtains and letting sunshine fill the room with light. She looked over at me, smiling. "Awake, are you, dearie? Well, you've had a good rest, and now I expect you'd like some breakfast. Dr. Barret left instructions before he went to make hospital rounds that I was to see you ate every bite." She brought a tray over to the bed and held it with one capable hand while I sat up, then with the other she plumped up the pillows behind my back.

"Oh, my, Miss Madison, that's a wicked bump you got on your head, turning quite purple it is now." She clucked her tongue, then stepped back from the bed, surveying me. "Dr. Barret also said to tell you he was stopping by Octagon House to let the folks there know about you."

It was obvious by the way she said it Mrs. Hammond did not feel too friendly toward my aunt's household.

Although my whole body ached and every muscle felt bruised, I was surprisingly hungry and quickly finished the bowl of hot porridge sprinkled with maple sugar, two applesauce muffins, and a cup of hot tea.

My arms were too stiff to raise, so Mrs. Hammond brushed my hair for me and braided it in one long plait over my shoulder.

"Doctor says you're to stay in bed until he gives you permission to get up," Mrs. Hammond said as she went out of the room with the breakfast tray.

Left alone I tried to recall the details of the day before. It was so bizarre. For a day that had started out with such gaiety to end in a near-fatal accident and to find myself — of all places — at Jordan's house seemed a weird twist of fate.

Jordan had been so gentle, so concerned, so tender as he had taken care of me and bandaged my foot. The doubts and uncertainties I had so recently harbored about him seemed groundless now.

Yet I was sure I hadn't been mistaken when I'd noticed how upset Jordan had become at the possibility of my aunt changing her will. Had my aunt promised something to Jordan that would be threatened by that?

Before I could get much further with this

line of thought, I heard the front door open and shut, Mrs. Hammond's cheerful greeting to Jordan, and the murmur of his reply. At the sound of his voice I felt my face grow hot, and my heart gave an excited little lurch.

Then Jordan appeared at the bedroom door. "So, how is my patient?" he asked with mock severity.

"Much better and very grateful," I murmured. "I cannot imagine what might have happened if it hadn't been your doorstep I stumbled onto last night — I don't think I could have taken another step."

He came over to the bed and casually picked up my hand, his fingers circled my wrist, taking my pulse. Not fair, I thought, knowing it had accelerated the minute he walked into the room.

"Are you ready to talk about what happened? I mean what *really* happened?" His eyes observed me clinically. "The explanations I got at Octagon House were pretty garbled and unbelievable."

As briefly and undramatically as possible I described my accident. "It was so silly and so strange, actually. I don't understand how it could have happened and nobody saw me —" I halted, frowning as I tried to remember exactly what happened right before I found myself spinning into space over the quarry.

"What is it, Julie?" Jordan asked.

"Oh, it was just — I probably only imagined it —"

"What?"

The horrible panic I had felt yesterday swept over me again, and I shuddered involuntarily. "After the accident, when I was trying to find my way back, I had the feeling that someone was following me — chasing me, actually — but it was probably the wind blowing the trees. That's when I fell. . . ." I stammered, feeling foolish at such an inconclusive recital.

Jordan did not speak for a moment, then he asked, "Doesn't it seem odd that neither Elvira nor Toby was concerned enough about you to look for you? That both of them went home from the hill alone — Elvira through the woods to Octagon House, Toby along the road? Toby says he saw your sled veer to one side as he went past, and thought you landed in a snowdrift, but he insists he had no idea you were in any sort of trouble. He went home via the Woodvale Tavern," Jordan added wryly. "Elvira says she decided *not* to take another ride and went back to the house without waiting for you to come back up the hill. Says she expected that when you got to the bottom of the hill, you'd walk back from there instead of climbing the hill again."

"Well, that does sound reasonable," I said slowly.

"Maybe reasonable enough, but I'm not convinced," Jordan said grimly. "Why are you making excuses for them, for their carelessness and lack of concern?" He paused, riveting his penetrating eyes on me. "I don't think you realize that if you hadn't somehow managed to drag yourself here, you could have frozen to death out there. Or worse still you could have landed at the bottom of the stone quarry smashed to bits —"

"Please, Jordan, don't!" I put both hands up as if to ward off the picture he was describing.

"I'm sorry, Julie; I'm simply trying to get you to see things as they are — or *may* be. I don't think it *was* your imagination. I think it might very well be that someone *was* following you — someone who wished you harm."

"Oh, no, Jordan!" I was aghast. "Who?"

"How long has it been since you've seen your cousins? Been in touch with them?" he demanded seriously.

"Years, actually. We haven't been together since —" I thought back. Elvira had left the winter before Toby and I were sent away to boarding school. "It must be eight years at least."

"Were you close then — as children, I mean?"

I nodded. "We accepted each other. After all, we were all in the same boat — half-orphans. All rebels against Aunt Octavia."

"A lot can happen to people, shifting their loyalties, altering their perspectives. From what you've told me about the Vale estate and you being chosen to inherit everything — that's a powerful motive for someone to want you out of the way."

I felt a jolt of shock. Jordan was putting into words the same thought I had had on that snowy hillside. A thought forged by dozens of memories when my two cousins had proved more enemies than allies. I now had to admit the possibility that one of them *might* mean me harm.

"But yesterday *had* to be an accident," I protested. "It couldn't have been planned —"

"Maybe it wasn't premeditated — maybe someone just seized the opportunity," Jordan said dryly.

I stared at him not wanting to accept his conclusion or my own.

"Don't you see what's at stake here Julie? Whoever controls the Vale estate is in charge of a fortune. Don't you realize that puts you in a very vulnerable position?"

As he said this I realized I had not had a chance to tell Jordan I had turned down Aunt Octavia's offer. My head began to ache fiercely. My expression must have shown this because Jordan said contritely, "Look, I'm sorry I've upset you, Julie. But I've seen first hand what dangling an inheritance in front of someone can do. Even the Bible warns us of the danger — 'the *love* of money is the root of all evil.' There are a handful of people to whom a fortune like the Vales' would mean a great deal. If they thought it was about to be snatched away from them, they'd be willing to do anything to keep it from happening."

In spite of myself I thought of Toby's debts, Elvira and her husband teetering on the brink of bankruptcy, even Ingersoll anxious about a comfortable pension in her old age for all the years of devotion.

Jordan got up and walked over to the door. "I have to go now; office hours begin in a few minutes. Try to get some rest. You shouldn't put any weight on the foot for a few days. I'd like you to stay here, where I could look out for you, where you'd be safe — but your aunt insisted that she was sending her carriage for you this afternoon. She said what was the use of having a trained nurse in residence if she had no one to take care of? So I guess you'll have to submit to Ingersoll's gentle ministrations." He looked amused. "But I'll come by Octagon House later to see you — as a patient, of course."

After Jordan left, his use of the word "safe" haunted me. Was my dread of returning to Octagon House more a premonition of danger? A deep inner dread took hold of me. As long as *anyone* believed I was willing to accept it, the Vale inheritance hung over me like the sword of Damocles.

Chapter Twenty

That afternoon Aunt Octavia sent the carriage she kept at the livery stable in Woodvale driven by Tim, whom she employed part-time, to take me back to Octagon House. Jordan followed in his small buggy, and he insisted on carrying me inside. Marshall opened the door for us, and as we started up the stairway to my room, Toby came bursting out from the parlor and Elvira came running down the third-floor stairway. Both followed us into my room, eager to explain and apologize for their actions on the day of the accident.

Listening to them, I had to agree with Jordan's impressions, that their explanations seemed too facile, too pat. But feeling weaker than I had expected, I did not want to prolong the discussion and was glad when Miss Ingersoll appeared and started asking Jordan professional questions about my condition.

"There's still some risk of lung congestion, and she's running a low fever. Her sprained ankle is swollen and painful. The best thing is for her to rest. I'll come around this evening to check on her."

"I'll see that your orders are carried out," she said primly.

Meekly, Elvira and Toby backed out of the room.

I wanted to protest that I didn't need or want Miss Ingersoll hovering, but Jordan was already digging into his medical bag, saying, "The important thing is to get her fever down, Nurse. I'll leave these powders for her to take if her ankle gives her too much pain, and here's something you can give her if she has trouble sleeping."

Jordan leaned down to me, saying gently, "I'll be back later, Julie. Try to get some rest and stay off that foot." After that, he left accompanied by Miss Ingersoll.

I can't remember ever having felt so tired. The exertion of dressing and coming back over to Octagon House had taken more effort than I realized. I wanted to try to think about some of the things Jordan had talked about, the questions he had raised about my cousins, make some plans. But my mind was dull and floating. I couldn't seem to hold on to a single idea. It must be the fever, I thought. Everything just sort of drifted away. . . .

I don't know how long I slept, but when I awakened the room was totally dark, the house silent. I was desperately thirsty but still felt almost too weak to move. I was lying there debating if I could gather the necessary energy to get up and get some water when the bedroom door creaked open. The dim light from the hallway outlined a woman's tall figure.

"Julie, are you awake?" It was Elvira.

"Yes, come in."

"Lutie made you some lemonade before she left, and I told her I'd bring it up to you when you woke up. It's after nine o'clock," she said as she set the tray she was carrying on the bureau. "How do you feel?"

"Better, I think. But I *am* thirsty."

"As soon as I get this lamp lighted so I can see, I'll pour you some lemonade," she said. She fumbled for matches in the little glass top hat kept beside the globed oil lamp on the table. The swish of the flame as the wick ignited sent shadows dancing on the wall and ceiling. Quickly Elvira replaced the glass chimney and turned back to the bureau, and I heard the splash of liquid into glass.

I bunched the pillows up behind my head and painfully sat up.

"Here." Elvira handed me a tumbler of

230

lemonade, and I sipped it. It tasted cool and tart and refreshing.

Elvira stood at the foot of the bed surveying me. "Jordan came by earlier, but when he heard you were sleeping, he decided he didn't want to disturb you. He *did* go up to see Aunt Octavia, though, and stayed up there for nearly a half hour."

I was both disappointed and relieved not to have seen Jordan. My feelings about him were so confused, and I had not had a chance to sort them out yet.

"Do you feel like talking?" Elvira asked, and without waiting for an answer she sat down at the end of the bed. "Julie, Toby and I feel just awful about what happened. If I'd had any idea you'd had an accident, I never would have left the hill. Please believe that. I thought you two were crazy to go on sledding when it was getting so cold and late. So I started down the other side of the hill. I came home, went upstairs, and took a nap. It wasn't until I came down to dinner that I found out what had happened." She paused. "And that Toby, I guess you know what he did when he got to the bottom of the hill after his last ride, don't you? He walked straight over to the Woodvale Tavern and had a few before he came home. By that time Jordan had sent word about you."

231

"Well, I'm all right, Elvira, I guess 'All's well that ends well,' " I said, trying not to think of the suspicious suggestions Jordan had made.

"Well, you should have heard Aunt Octavia's reaction. She sent for Toby and me as if we were two infants! She lashed us up and down as only she can. Told us how utterly stupid and childish we'd all been to go out sledding in the first place. We already felt bad enough, but, of course, she had to go on and on about it."

"I'm sorry, Elvira," I murmured.

"After that, Toby and I stayed up half the night talking." She paused. "Did you have any idea what he's been doing all these years? Playing piano in sleazy dance halls and saloons! Besides gambling away all the money that was supposed to be spent on his musical education. Wouldn't Aunt Octavia have a fit if she knew — but then, she probably does. She had us all followed by private investigators — at least, that's what she says. I don't know whether to believe that or not. Aunt Octavia would use any means to achieve what she wants. And Toby and I both agree she wanted *you* to be the sole inheritor from the beginning. That neither of us ever really had a chance —"

"But, Elvira, I told you —"

"Julie, Uncle Victor thinks so, too. He came in while we were discussing it, and he said he had always taken it for granted. But he thought one of us should talk to Aunt Octavia again and point out the only fair thing to do would be to make some kind of equitable settlement on us *now* — for our Vale parents' sake."

Elvira got off the bed and moved over to the window. I could see her profile in the light cast by the lamp; it looked harsh and sharp against the white curtains.

"So? Did you?" I asked.

"Yes, fool that I was. The result was another terrible scene — a shouting match. I lost my temper again. It's so unfair. It really is. Not that I blame you, Julie, but it *is* —"

An officious little rat-a-tat-tat came at my door, then it opened and Miss Ingersoll came in. I had the instinctive feeling she had been standing outside listening. She gave Elvira a disapproving look as she came over to my bedside.

"I've brought the powders Dr. Barret prescribed for you, Miss Madison. You're to take one before you go to sleep, and I'll leave another on your table here in case you wake up during the night. Shall I fix it for you?"

"No, thank you, Miss Ingersoll, I'm drinking this lemonade now, and I've just awakened. I'm not ready to go to sleep yet," I said.

"Well, be sure you do take it. Doctor's orders, miss." She looked annoyed that I had refused. Then she glanced around at Elvira and said, "I don't think Miss Madison ought to be stimulated with a lot of conversation. Talking's not good for someone with a fever."

Elvira did not bother to reply, just gave Miss Ingersoll a saccharinely sweet smile, her "Cheshire cat smile," Toby and I used to call it. Affronted that her professional advice was being ignored, Miss Ingersoll swept out of the room, her chin jutting out belligerently. Elvira made a face and stuck out her tongue at the departing figure.

"What a beast she is. I wonder how Aunt Octavia has put up with her all these years. Someone to bully, I suppose." She came back over to the bed again. "As I was saying, Julie, I tried to present our case — Toby's and mine — calmly and rationally, but she would not give an inch! She actually shouted at me and got so angry I became alarmed. I was actually afraid she was having some kind of seizure."

"Oh, Elvira!" I exclaimed. "Jordan says her blood pressure is dangerously high —"

"Well, anyway, Toby was standing outside

234

in the hallway, ready to come in and supply reinforcement — safety in numbers, you know — because at one time we had thought, remember, that *he* was her favorite. Well, when he came in, it only made matters worse. She castigated us both. Said as long as she was alive we'd never get a penny of the Vale money, and she was going to make sure that *after her death*, the terms of her new will would make it impossible. She has Ross Holden drawing it up now; she told us he was bringing it for her signature tomorrow."

I shook my head. "It's all wrong, Elvira. But I have done everything I know to convince her that I don't want —"

"It's no use, Julie, she doesn't accept that." Elvira tossed her head. "Anyway, when Toby and I left the room, Ingersoll and Marshall were in some kind of deep confab in the hall, so I know they heard every word. Toby and I went back downstairs to discuss it further but finally came to the conclusion that it was hopeless." She paused again. "We're both leaving. I had Marshall bring down my luggage from the attic, and I've already started packing. Toby's going to check tomorrow to see if the trains are back on schedule; by now the tracks should be clear."

"Oh, Elvira, don't go!" I begged, suddenly panic-stricken at the thought of being left alone at Octagon House, especially incapacitated.

"Why should I stay, Julie?" She shrugged. "I dread telling Drew my mission was a failure." She sighed deeply, then put her hands up on either side of her head, massaging her temples with her long, thin fingers. "Of course, I have a migraine coming on; I should have known all this stress would do it." She stood up and, steadying herself by grasping the bedpost, asked, "Do you think I could possibly take that prescription Jordan left for you? He said it was a pain-killer, didn't he? And this pain is vicious."

"I guess it would be all right," I said rather hesitantly.

"I don't want to have to go ask Ingersoll for anything. I'd almost rather be scorching in hell than ask *her* for a drop of water. It's obvious she detests us all — even Toby!"

Elvira picked up one of the small packets Miss Ingersoll had placed on the bedside table. "Take as needed for pain" was written on it in Jordan's handwriting.

"Thanks, Julie," Elvira said, pocketing it. At my door she turned and asked, "Can I do anything for you before I go?"

I shook my head. "Except, maybe —

Elvira, couldn't you and Toby wait until my ankle's healed, and then we could all leave at the same time?"

She frowned, looking doubtful. "I don't know, Julie. I've written out a telegram for Toby to leave at the wireless office to send to Drew; he'll be expecting me —"

"Do think about it, Elvira, reconsider. . . ."

"Well, let's see what tomorrow brings," she said. Her hand went up to her head again, and I knew I shouldn't delay her any longer. "Good night, Julie, sweet dreams — if anything like that is possible in *this* house!" she said as she went out.

Sweet dreams? I echoed to myself smiling a little at Elvira's ironic humor.

Hours later, still lying sleepless, I might have welcomed *any* kind, sweet or otherwise, to escape my troubled thoughts. Sleep stubbornly evaded me. Yet for some reason I resisted taking the sleeping powder Jordan had left. I needed to be clear-headed to decide what to do. If only I could leave at once. Unconsciously I moved my foot, and a sharp, hot twist of pain zigzagged from my ankle up my leg, reminding me that escape without help was impossible. My worst nightmare had become a reality — I was trapped here at Octagon House indefinitely.

Gradually the gray light of dawn stole in

through the windows, and I realized resignedly that another day at Octagon House was beginning. Why had I ever come back here? I asked myself endlessly. I could have remained quietly in the small college town, maybe even married Francis Wilburn, the mild history professor for whom I'd done research work. Why had I allowed myself to be drawn back to this house, haunted by its old secrets, and to a man as complicated, difficult, and puzzling as Jordan?

Was it true that even our smallest decisions dictate our destiny?

From the moment I had arrived I seemed to have been entangled in the mysteries of Octagon House and unable to extricate myself.

Suddenly I heard movement outside my bedroom door. I tensed. Who was prowling the halls at this hour? Then, slowly, my door was opened, and I saw the outline of a shadowy figure hunched in the threshold. A scream lodged in my throat as it shuffled into the room.

"Who is it?" I whispered hoarsely.

The figure stumbled forward toward my bed, and I shrank back, bracing myself for an attack, when to my relief I saw it was Elvira. Then I looked at her, horrified. She looked like one of the witches from *Macbeth*, her red hair streaming down each side of her face, whose pallor had a ghastly greenish tinge.

"Elvira! What's the matter? You look like death!"

With one shaky hand she pushed back her hair, and through swollen, cracked lips she rasped, "I am almost — dead! I've been horribly ill. I came to warn *you*. Whatever you do, *don't* take any of those powders Jordan left for you. They're poison."

Chapter Twenty-one

Shocked, I stared at my cousin.

"What do you mean? What are you saying?"

Elvira looked at me from her sunken eyes. "I'm telling you what happened, Julie. It's only a miracle I didn't take the whole dosage!" she said, shuddering and shaking her head. "I emptied part of the package into a glass of water, then somehow I bumped my elbow and spilled half of it. I filled the glass up again with water and then swallowed it." She clutched my arm with both hands. "If I'd taken it *all* — I'd be dead, I'm sure of it!"

But the powder had been meant for *me*. I didn't even have to say it; I could see my own dismaying realization confirmed in her wide-eyed stare.

"But *why?*" I asked.

"Oh, Julie, don't you see? Don't you understand *yet?*" Elvira demanded wearily. "Someone wants you out of the way — *per-*

manently. You are the stumbling block to someone's inheritance. Whoever it is, is not taking any chances that Aunt Octavia will change her will in favor of you and cut them out!"

"But who besides *us* — you, Toby, me, and Uncle Victor — knows she has chosen me?"

"*Everyone* knows it. Don't you realize there are no secrets at Octagon House, maybe no secrets in Woodvale?" Her grip tightened on my arm. "I'm going to get Toby to take what's left of the powder in the packet to the pharmacy and have it analyzed. It should be simple enough for a pharmacist to tell the difference between some kind of analgesic or bromide and — arsenic."

"Arsenic?" I gasped.

"Of course. Arsenic is easy enough to get. I know it's kept in the storeroom to kill rats! It's a white, powdery substance, no odor, no taste, apparently, although, I *did* think there was a slightly bitter aftertaste to the medicine, but, of course, I didn't think much of it at the time." She looked sick. "It's almost untraceable in small quantities. It's often used by murderers, given to victims in small doses over a period of time so they seem to be just suffering from some undiagnosed illness at first, then gradually they become totally deteriorated and eventually die a lingering death. And no one's the wiser. Except the murderer, of course, who's done his dastardly deed without detection."

"But that's horrible!" I exclaimed.

"Well, they'll not get away with it. Whoever it is . . ."

"Elvira, maybe you're wrong. Maybe you were just going to be sick anyway from your headache."

"Julie, I *know* the difference between a normal sick headache and what happened to me last night. Whether you want to believe it or not, you are in mortal danger — maybe from someone you trust!"

Shivering, Elvira gathered the cape around her and stood up. "I've got to lie down. I'll talk to Toby, tell him, I *know* he'll understand what we've got to do."

Elvira went back to her room to bed to try and recover from the violent nausea that had awakened her less than an hour after she had taken the prescription painkiller Jordan had left for *me*. After she left, there was no possibility of sleep for me. I huddled in bed with the covers up to my chin. Who wanted to kill me? Everyone seemed suspicious of someone else. Jordan suspected my cousins. Elvira suspected Jordan. But who had followed me that first early morning in the woods? Who had shoved my sled, sending me careening down the icy hillside to possible death?

The hours to daylight passed slowly. As the darkness faded I could see it had begun to rain. I heard its relentless beat on the overhang outside my bedroom windows, adding to my already depressive mood. One thought dominated everything else. Escape! I must leave Octagon House, before something terrible happened.

But the only way I could leave Octagon House without anyone knowing until after I was gone, was to go on foot. The swelling had gone down. My ankle was much better. And although it still hurt when I tried putting my weight on it, I would have to manage.

I practiced walking back and forth a few times. My mind worked feverishly. I would have to get my bags down from the attic in order to pack. I couldn't ask Marshall to bring them down without my intention of leaving being discovered.

I would stay in my room all day, pretending to be resting, then at night when everyone was asleep, I could sneak up to the attic, retrieve my suitcase, pack, and as soon as it was light, slip out of the house. Once on the road I might be able to hail an omnibus or a passing hansom cab. I would just have to take my chances. The important thing was to get to the train station and take the first train out, wherever it was headed.

Elvira had said it might take twenty-four hours to get a report back from the pharmacist on the powder. Then I remembered — Jordan had said he made up his own prescriptions!

I shuddered. No! Not Jordan! Surely Jordan would not want me to die!

But then people wore so many masks, there were so many hidden pieces in the maze surrounding Octagon House. How could I be sure that anything was as it appeared?

A sharp rap on my bedroom door startled me, and before I could even say "Come in," Miss Ingersoll bustled in with a breakfast tray.

At her entrance, I instinctively felt something evil enter the room with Miss Ingersoll. Or was it my imagination heightened by Elvira's dire warning?

I observed the nurse carefully. Miss Ingersoll seemed her usual crisp, professional self. Could this brisk, determinedly cheerful woman be a potential murderess? Or was she just an annoying busybody?

Somehow, as I watched her, the horror of Elvira's midnight visit began to lose its impact. Elvira was given to dramatics. Could she be wrong? Or did she have her own motives to try to influence me to flee Octagon House as if in danger of my life? That would narrow the field of inheritance to Toby and her, leaving *her* the obvious choice for the position *she* coveted.

I felt so confused, so frightened, so pressured by my own turbulent thoughts I did not hear what Miss Ingersoll said at first, and she had to repeat herself. "I'll take a look at that ankle now, miss; Doctor said it should be rebandaged."

"Oh, I don't think that will be necessary, thank you," I protested, but Miss Ingersoll ignored me.

"Tut, tut, Dr. Barret will be cross at me if I don't take good care of his patient," she said and got out a roll of gauze and whipped out her surgical scissors from the pocket of her starched apron. "Although, goodness knows, I have enough to do with Miss Vale, who is being twice as demanding as usual today." She pursed her mouth as she unwrapped the old bandage, then quickly and efficiently applied a new one. "Not too tight, is it? We wouldn't want to cut off the circulation."

"No, it's fine, thank you," I murmured.

245

"Would you like one of the painkiller powders now?" she asked, narrowing her eyes and surveying me closely.

"Oh, no!" I gasped, then hoped I hadn't sounded too startled.

"You're sure?"

"No, I mean, yes, thank you. I really am fine."

"Hmmph," was all she replied. Still hesitating, she moved uncertainly toward the door, then turned. "Well, then, if you're quite sure, I'll take my constitutional; I need to get out in the fresh air."

"But isn't it raining?" I asked, glancing out the window, where silver streaks of rain striped the windowpanes and dripped from the eaves.

"Rain or shine, out I go!" she replied firmly. "That's where I get my stamina, I never let weather keep me indoors."

After she went out of the room, I looked at the tray she had left for me. Did I dare eat anything? Surely if Lutie had fixed the food, it should be safe. However, Miss Ingersoll could have sprinkled something into the sugar, into the tea . . . couldn't she have?

I felt the cold sensation of fear overtake me. No, I had better not risk it.

Was I going out of my mind? Suspecting

everything and everybody? Or was I just being careful, as anyone whose life was in danger would be?

I reviewed all possible plans to get away. I would remain in my room all day, wait for the opportunity to sneak up to the attic. I couldn't plan any further than that.

As the day wore on, I got hungrier and hungrier. I pretended to be asleep when Miss Ingersoll knocked, then tiptoed in and took my tray. I was aware of movement deep in the house, voices, but no one came in to disturb me.

It was nearly evening when Elvira returned. Somehow, lulled by the monotonous sound of the rain, I had actually drifted off to sleep and was surprised at her entrance to find the room dark. She had brought her own lamp with her and set it on the bureau, then came over to my bed and shook my shoulder.

I sat up and looked at her. She was dressed and had done up her hair, but she still looked gaunt and pale.

"Julie!" she whispered hoarsely. "Toby wasn't able to get the powder analyzed. The pharmacist had gone home sick and only his assistant was there. Toby wasn't sure *he* could be trusted to keep it confidential, so he didn't leave it. We're just as much in the dark as ever, *except* —" Elvira paused significantly.

"Except what?"

"Well, Toby has a theory he's checking out further. . . ."

"What kind of a theory?"

"He thinks we're all *three* targets. As soon as it was known *we* were coming back here, the rumor spread that Aunt Octavia was going to change her will in favor of one of us. *Apparently,* this made some people very nervous, people who had thought that a big legacy was coming their way. That would be Aunt Octavia's style, hinting that she was leaving people large sums of money to manipulate them. Get them to do things she wanted done. Then the *three* of us, who haven't been seen or heard from in years, show up! *Voila!* We're a threat, a danger to anyone who was anticipating wealth. Solution? Get rid of us! Either frighten us away, or if that doesn't work, *kill* us off."

"But —"

"Listen, Julie, Toby didn't say anything about it before, but after I told him about the powder I suspect was poison, he told me that he was sure he had been followed several times from the Woodvale Tavern — the last time was the night of *your* accident. He had the definite feeling it was someone prepared to harm him. He said that whoever it

248

was, was gaining on him when he managed to hail down a farmer coming home from market and got a lift with him in his wagon."

"But *who* — ?" I began.

"It doesn't matter *who*, Julie, or whether it's more than one. I think he's right, we're all in danger." She lowered her voice. "When I told him about the possibility that arsenic was used and explained that it's odorless and practically tasteless, his eyes got wide and he turned pale. He says he got sick from some brandy he drank one night, the night after his awful row with Aunt Octavia. And Toby's used to drinking quite a lot and has never before been sick!"

When Elvira said this, I remembered my own bad reaction to the small amount of brandy I'd shared with Toby that night, and I recalled Lutie's remark about Toby having a dreadful hangover the next day. . . .

"So you *see!*" finished Elvira with an air of triumph, gratified at being correct even about something as horrible as attempted murder. "It could be *anyone*" — she hesitated, then said in a rush — "it could *even* be Jordan Barret!"

I felt my throat tighten. "Why, Jordan?"

Elvira lowered her voice conspiratorially. "Well, I was making some inquiries about the Vale estate, you remember? I went to the courthouse, to Ross Holden's office. I also went to the bank. And while I was waiting to see Mr. Franchot, the manager, I saw Jordan. He was talking to one of the loan officers. He didn't see me — he was in a pretty intense conversation — then later I saw him up at the cashier's window. I don't know if he was putting money in or —" Elvira raised her eyebrows — "maybe . . . getting a loan payoff? One thing I *do know* is that a country doctor is as poor as the proverbial church mouse. I'm sure he sometimes gets paid in potatoes or corn! What if Aunt Octavia had promised Jordan some large amount of money — and *then* we three show up?"

Elvira couldn't have said anything that would have shaken me more. I still recalled Jordan's reaction when he learned Aunt Octavia was planning to change her will. My next thought was — what was the second best thing to receiving a large legacy yourself? Marrying the heiress, of course!

I hated what I was thinking. But I couldn't get rid of the thought. "Oh, I wish I'd never come back here!" I cried out.

"So say we all! But we may still be able to thwart whoever planned this." Elvira paused, biting her lip nervously. "The best thing we can do for now is get a good night's sleep, and in the morning I think the three of us should go to Ross Holden and express our doubts about Aunt Octavia's mental state."

"What?"

"Well, she's obviously getting senile, Julie. Why else would she have come up with this impossible, unfair, unworkable plan for the estate? I think we can get enough evidence among us to prove her incompetent and have the three of us jointly declared conservators."

"Oh, Elvira, that's a dreadful thing to do!"

"Not any worse than what she's done to *us!*" Elvira retorted. "Don't forget our Vale parents were every bit as much Clement Vale's children as she and Uncle Victor are, and we have a right to an equitable distribution of the estate."

I didn't say anything. But I knew I was not going to be a party to having Aunt Octavia, whom I knew to be as sane as anyone, declared incompetent. Elvira and Toby could do what they wanted. I was getting out. I knew now I couldn't confide my plan to Elvira. So I said nothing more, and in a few minutes she left.

I felt terribly alone. There was no one I could depend on, no one I could trust. Whatever happened now I had to act on my own.

I thought of all the subconscious signals I'd received from the time I received Aunt Octavia's letter, all the small, persistent misgivings, warnings *not* to accept the invitation, not to come, and I'd ignored them all.

Foolishly, recklessly, I'd returned to a place where I'd known unhappiness and heartbreak. I had no one to blame but myself for the dangerous dilemma I was in now.

I heard the clock strike downstairs. Soon the house would settle down for the night. Then, and only then, dared I attempt the first part of my plan.

Chapter Twenty-two

Gradually the house quieted for the night. I'd pushed a chair over to my bedroom door, where I'd perched, listening, for what seemed like hours. I'd heard the doorbell ring once and limped silently to the third-floor balcony but had only seen Marshall making his nightly rounds and locking up.

Finally, by midnight, everything was still. The plan that had seemed so plausible all day suddenly seemed crazy. My thinking seemed disorganized. What would they all think when they found me gone tomorrow? Should I wait and act in conjunction with my cousins? Then I thought of the way I'd been shoved down the hill on my sled and left to die or find my way back alone in the freezing winter night, of the possibly poisoned powders — No, there was nobody I could be sure of, no one I could trust absolutely. Both Elvira and Toby were able to act upon their own if they, too, felt threatened. Maybe *I* was deluded, but I could not take the chance that I was wrong.

While I hesitated, vacillated, the bonging of the hall clock struck the quarter hour. There had been no sound or movement for an endless stretch of time, and yet I waited. Why was I so hesitant? The door leading up to the attic was just at the end of the third-floor hall, only a short distance. I could make it there and back with my suitcase in a matter of minutes — even with my bad ankle. What would I say if someone woke up and saw me? Nonsense, I told myself. In my bare feet I could move soundlessly down the carpeted hallway, with no one the wiser until morning. After I was discovered gone, Elvira would understand; Toby, too, eventually.

I sashed my challis robe over my nightgown, put a candle and some matches into the pocket, then eased open my bedroom door and slipped out into the hall. My ankle gave some twinges as I tiptoed toward the attic door. Upon reaching it I unconsciously looked over my shoulder. Cautiously I turned the knob, but as I inched open the door, its hinges creaked. I held my breath. But even though it had sounded loud to me, evidently no one else had heard it. I opened the door wider and went through.

The attic stairs were steep and narrow. I

took them carefully one at a time, hoping they would not squeak under my weight. Not wanting to light the candle until I reached the top, I had to feel my way up by putting my hands on the walls on either side. It was slow going; I kept tripping over the hem of my nightgown.

At the last step I felt the wooden floor with my hands and sighed with relief. So far, so good. I paused to strike one of the matches and lit the candle. Its faint flame shed light on only a small section of the attic at a time. This proved a problem because the attic was huge, running the width and length of the floor below, its low, slanted ceiling forming the octagon shape of the roof. I held the candle high as I turned around slowly, trying to see where Marshall had placed our luggage.

Looking around the cavernous room, I was amazed at the number of things stored up here. The household furnishings stacked and piled into the corners gathering dust would be enough for two other homes. There were also dozens of boxes and wooden crates standing about.

Hot wax dripping on my fingers alerted me that my candle was burning fast, and I must hurry before it went out. But I couldn't locate my suitcase. I turned this way and that, sending the flickering beam of my candle around. Suddenly I heard the door to the attic creak open. Then to my horror I heard footsteps approaching on the stairs.

I blew out my candle in panic and pressed myself against the nearest wall. What should I do? Where could I go? With less than a minute to decide I moved along the wall, my hands fumbling for a place to hide. My eyes, newly accustomed to the dark, searched frantically for an empty space. Then I saw the outline of an old-fashioned humped-back trunk and quickly crouched down behind it out of sight.

The wavering light from an oil lamp appeared at the top of the steps. I wasn't able to see who held it. I raised my eyes above the top of the trunk, peered over, and saw the figure of a man carrying something bulky covered in cloth. He set the lamp down on one of the wooden crates, and at last I saw who it was.

Marshall! I had mistakenly assumed that after he had locked up the house, he had retired to his apartment over the carriage barn. In amazement I watched him unwrap the swathed object. When I saw it was one of the eight-branched silver candlesticks that were always on the mahogany sideboard in the dining room, I suppressed a gasp. He pulled forward a wooden crate, slid off the top, pushed aside mounds of excelsior, and then carefully placed the candelabra down into it. He covered it with more excelsior, then started to put the lid back on the box.

I was stunned. Marshall, the trusted family servant for years, obviously stealing valuables. Then something else clicked in my brain. Of course! *He* was the mysterious "agent" bringing artifacts to sell secretly to the antique shop in Perrysville, pretending he was acting for Aunt Octavia because she needed money, then probably pocketing the price himself! That's what had happened to the missing porcelain dogs! The realization made me almost angry enough to stand up and confront him then and there.

But before I had time to do anything more than absorb all this, I saw Marshall turn his head quickly as if startled. He got up from his knees and took a few steps toward the attic steps just as Miss Ingersoll's head emerged from the stairs.

"Well, Marshall, what are you doing?" she asked sarcastically.

Marshall seemed to take a moment to compose himself, then he asked in an equally sarcastic tone, "I could ask the same of you, except I *know* — spying, as usual."

Miss Ingersoll gave a shrill little laugh and folded her arms across her flat chest. "I admit I heard something and investigated, then decided to follow you up here. Actually, I've had my eye on you for quite a while, Marshall. I've suspected you were up to something like this. How do you explain stealing valuables from your employer?"

"*Stealing?* I wouldn't call it that. I'd simply call it insurance against a destitute old age, avoiding being thrown out with the trash once Miss Octavia is gone," Marshall replied smoothly, then added, "Besides, the old lady will never miss these things. You've said yourself she's getting forgetful. Until the three of *them* came she hadn't even been downstairs in the dining or drawing rooms for a long time."

"Oh, I knew you'd try to justify yourself," Miss Ingersoll sneered. "Always so high and mighty, aren't you? And it turns out you're just a common thief!"

"At least I'm not a *fool,* like some I know, expecting to be remembered in her will." He finished with a harsh laugh.

The strong light from her lamp sent deep shadows onto Miss Ingersoll's face as it twisted with wrath. Almost instantly her anger was replaced by fear, which widened her curiously light gray-green eyes. "I'm no fool, Marshall," she denied. "*She* promised me, as did old Mrs. Vale. I have her word for it; she told me if I stayed with her, I'd never have to worry —"

"Ha! Is it in writing? I wouldn't count on it. I've been with this family for years, you know. People like the Vales don't keep promises. Other people exist only for their convenience, like furniture. I learned that long ago." He shrugged indifferently.

"I've given the Vales my life, my youth, my chances . . . first Mrs. Vale and now Miss Octavia," Miss Ingersoll said heatedly. "I don't intend to be cheated out of what's due me."

"You poor idiot!" Marshall shook his head at her. "Don't you know she's planning to change her will? So whatever she said before *they* came, you can forget. One of them is getting it all."

"That shows how much *you* know, Marshall. I didn't leave it all to chance or count only on promises. I'm making *sure* I'll get what's coming to me, *no matter what*." Her expression remained smug.

Marshall eyed her warily. "Don't do anything stupid, Ingersoll. I'm only taking what's rightfully mine after all these years. These things will never be missed, but they will provide me with a comfortable old age."

He spoke calmly with assurance.

Miss Ingersoll looked somewhat disconcerted. "You could get caught, you know. *I* could turn you in myself," she said.

Marshall just laughed and shoved the wooden crate with his foot. He dusted the residue from the excelsior from his hands and the knees of his trousers.

"And I could tell Miss Octavia where all the bottles of her rare vintage wine keep disappearing to, couldn't I?" he snarled. "You'd be out of here in two seconds if she knew her nurse was a secret tippler, now wouldn't you? And then where would you go, what would you do? No reputable hospital would hire a nurse who drinks on the sly."

Miss Ingersoll looked uncomfortable, but she gave her head a little toss. "That's nothing to taking priceless silver and china and reselling them! You could be put in jail for something like that!"

All at once Marshall straightened, listening. "What was *that?*"

"I didn't hear anything."

"Sounded like the front doorbell. I thought —" Marshall swore under his breath. "I suppose it's Mr. Victor; the old codger's probably forgotten his key again. I'll have to go let him in." He brushed past

Miss Ingersoll and went down the steps.

I held my breath, hoping Miss Ingersoll would go, too. But the nurse had picked up her lamp and was looking around curiously. She went over to the box Marshall had just shut and pushed back the top to look inside. While she was thus occupied, I tried to shift my cramped position, but my ankle gave way and I lost my balance. I fell back against some loosely stacked cardboard boxes, and they thudded to the floor.

Miss Ingersoll whirled around, swinging her lamp in a wide circle, and its light caught me as I scrambled to right myself. Immediately Miss Ingersoll's startled expression changed to anger. "What are *you* doing here?" she spat at me like an enraged cat.

Hampered by my nightgown, which had tangled with the heavier cloth of my robe, I struggled to pull myself up, but Miss Ingersoll was beside me before I could get to my feet.

"You little sneak," she hissed as her fingers bit into the flesh of my arm. "How much did you hear?"

"I just came up to find my suitcase — I was frightened when I heard Marshall coming, I didn't know, I —" I stammered, not knowing what to say.

Miss Ingersoll's face underwent another quick change. This time from fury to a kind of sardonic satisfaction that was even more intimidating. "Your suitcase, eh? Coming up here to get your suitcase? Planning to leave, Miss Madison? Well — what a coincidence. One that could be turned to my advantage . . ." Her pale eyes glittered maliciously. "Going to leave, were you? What a good idea! You've played right into my plans, miss."

With that the nurse yanked me up roughly. My weight was thrown onto my injured foot, and I cried out in pain. She paid no attention; she was surprisingly strong and she shoved me in front of her. She was talking in a monotone, almost as if to herself.

"*I'll* find your suitcase and pack it for you. Yes, this will all work out nicely. I already have the notes you wrote to Dr. Barret; I found them on your desk in your room. That was careless, just leaving them out so anyone could read them. And I did! You said you were going away. We'll just see that the letter is delivered after you disappear, and no one will guess. They won't find you — not for years — no one comes up here but Marshall on his private errands. But now that I've found him out, I don't think he'll be coming again soon — and when he does, it will be too late for you, miss."

"Please, Miss Ingersoll, I don't intend to say anything to Aunt Octavia about anything — about Marshall or —" I hardly knew what I was saying, trying only to calm the irrational anger I could feel in her.

"Oh, no, miss, you won't be telling anyone anything, not for a while — not for a very long while — I'll see to *that*. Go on, get in there," she ordered and yanked open the door to the cupola.

Terror stricken, I shrank back, resisting. All my horrible childhood memories, my fear of enclosed places and of heights assailed me.

"Oh, no, not in there, please. . . ." I protested.

Her hand closed like a vise around my arm, and she thrust me forward so that I fell in a crumpled heap on the cupola floor. I tried to struggle up, but Miss Ingersoll pulled out her surgical scissors from the pocket of her apron and held them over me threateningly.

"Get back!" she said between clenched teeth. Then she slammed the door shut. I heard the lock turn.

I dragged myself up just in time to see through the cracks of warped door the last wavering light of Miss Ingersoll's lamp disappear as she went down the stairway, and closed that door as well.

I was left in total darkness. I was too shocked at the speed in which all this had happened to react right away. Then, slowly, sickeningly, it penetrated that I was trapped here, in this cramped, unheated cubbyhole at the base of the cupola. Left here to freeze or starve to death . . . to die.

Chapter Twenty-three

Above me the wind whistled eerily, rattling the windows of the cupola. I leaned against the door into the attic as hard as I could running my hands all over the wood. Then with horror I remembered the cupola door only had a handle on the attic side. From the cupola side it pushed open easily unless — unless the sturdy wooden bolt was slid across locking it securely.

I realized I was in the exact same situation I'd been in when I was a little girl and Toby and Elvira had locked me in here. There was no way to get out unless someone came up here and found me.

Slowly I sank down to the floor. All the old childish horror of being closed in, high above the rest of the house, with no hope of escape, paralyzed me.

Should I call out, scream, bang on the door? Would any such cry for help be heard from here at the top of this house with its many rooms and thick walls and doors?

Could Miss Ingersoll actually get anyone to believe her fantastic story about me? Wouldn't Elvira be suspicious? Surely she wouldn't believe I would leave without telling *her*, after all we had discussed? The letters, I thought with a pang of regret. All those ones I'd started to Jordan, saying I couldn't stay another night under the roof at Octagon House. Of course, that was how Miss Ingersoll knew *I* was the one Aunt Octavia had chosen to be sole inheritor.

I remembered the day I'd come upstairs and found her at the door of my bedroom. She had made some excuse, but now I saw through it all. She had been in there then poking around, seeing what she could find.

A freezing sliver of cold sliced through me. I shivered, drawing my light robe closer. There must be a broken window in the cupola letting in the winter night's frigid air. I tucked my bare feet under my nightgown, trying to warm them even as the bone-chilling damp of this unheated part of the house pierced through me.

I heard scuttling sounds. Rats? I shuddered with revulsion. I recalled Elvira saying she knew arsenic was kept here at Octagon House to control rats. The thought of being shut up in here with rats made me ill. I got to my feet and began banging on the door in a mindless frenzy.

Only silence met my frantic beating; my fists stung with the effort and a sob caught raggedly in my throat. Just then I became aware that it had begun to rain harder, the heavy drops beating on the glass sides of the cupola, drowning out any cry of mine.

I moaned in frustration. Helpless tears poured down my face, but I angrily wiped them away. What good did it do to cry? I had to *think*, figure a way to get help, be rescued.

That other time, years ago, when I'd been locked in here, my childish hysteria had resulted in my lying whimpering on the floor at the base of the winding cupola stairs, my throat raw from screaming, my little fists bloody and bruised from beating on the door.

That whole episode came back to me in detail. The day had been gloomy, a rainy winter afternoon. Both Aunt Octavia and Uncle Victor had gone out, the servants occupied in the lower part of the house, the three of us restless and bored. Elvira had suggested a game of hide-and-seek, and while she counted, Toby and I had scattered, each scouting for the best place to hide.

We weren't supposed to go up past the

third floor, but we often did. Once when we'd gone up to explore, we found the door leading up to the attic. Elvira had scared Toby and me with ghost stories about old murders that had supposedly taken place there. The one I particularly remembered was about a skeleton found hanging in the cupola.

I guess in the exhilaration of the game that day, I momentarily forgot the scary stories. I had merely decided the cupola would be the best hiding place. I was sure no one would find me there.

Of course, that's exactly what happened. After hiding quite awhile without anyone finding me, I decided to go back downstairs. That's when I discovered there was no way to get out. The door locked from outside; there was no inner handle.

When I didn't appear at suppertime, Lutie had gone on a search and found me terrified in the cupola.

I never knew who locked me in; both Elvira and Toby denied doing it. Each said they had grown tired of the game when they couldn't find me and gone their separate ways to other amusements.

But I had too often been the target of Elvira's petty cruelties and of Toby's mischief to believe either of them. I was sure one of them had followed me up there, hidden until I went into the cupola, then sneaked up and locked the door thinking it would be a great joke. The experience had made an indelible mark on me, leaving me with a morbid dread of small enclosured spaces as well as a fear of heights.

And that is what faced me now. If I climbed up to the top into the cupola and lit my candle, perhaps someone passing on the road might see me and send someone to investigate and alert the household. Whatever the chances, I had to try something. I didn't think I could stay sane if I had to stay shut up in here.

Desperate situations require desperate action. That garbled quote came to mind as I stiffened my resolve to do whatever it took to secure rescue. I fumbled for the matches in the pocket of my robe and tried striking one on the floor to light what was left of my candle. The first match flared briefly, then went out. I lit a second and cupped my hand around it to protect the flame, then tilted my candle until the wick caught fire. The illumination was meager, but enough for me to see a little.

I stood and examined the way up to the cupola. The staircase was little more than a circular metal ladder. I gathered my nightgown and robe, bunched them up, and thrust them through the sash of my robe to free my lower legs and feet. Holding the candle in one shaky hand, gripping the tubular handrail with the other, I started up.

Taking one step at a time with my good foot, then bringing my injured one up after, I mounted, breathing hard, heart thudding, cold sweat beading my forehead and trickling down my back. Higher and higher I went around the twisting, wobbly staircase which seemed to tremble with each step I took.

Don't let me panic and fall, I prayed. My hand was clammy and kept slipping on the railing, but at last I saw the windows of the cupola, shiny and glistening with rain. Out of breath I reached the top. The wax was dripping all over my fingers as the candle burned low. Would it last? Would it even be seen in the rain if I held it aloft and waved it back and forth in a signal for help?

My bundled nightgown and robe had come loose and were hampering my progress, but I didn't dare let go the rail to grab them again. Stumbling, I turned myself into a sitting position on the floor of the cupola and slid back from the steps. I twisted my body, crawled from the edge of the stairs, and finally staggered to my feet.

I drew a long, shaking breath. I'd done it. I was in the cupola. I felt dizzy. I mustn't think of how high it was, I told myself. The candle flame was sinking lower, the candle dripping wax on my fingers.

Through the rain-misted glass I figured out which side of the cupola faced the road. That's where I should stand to wave the candle. Even as I began, I felt the hopelessness of the effort. Who in the world would be passing Octagon House so late on a night as rainswept as this?

Telling myself firmly that my efforts were not in vain, I moved the candle back and forth rhythmically. Even though I could see nothing in the darkness below, I dared not despair. Perhaps someone passing by on the road might see this flickering light; I knew it was almost an automatic reflex of people to look up at the oddly structured mansion as they went by. I prayed tonight someone would do just that and be curious enough to investigate.

But with the rumors that Octagon House was haunted, the light might be thought some kind of ghostly apparition wafting up in the cupola! Perhaps all I was doing was scaring away any passersby. My arm grew tired, and the futility of what I was doing soon discouraged me. Who could possibly see this single flickering candle through the curtain of rain?

My candle was almost a stub, my hand covered with melted wax, when all at once I saw the pale yellow orbs of carriage lights turn into the gate of Octagon House. Frantically I flashed my candle, but the movement stirred the air, and suddenly my candle went out.

My heart sank. What could I do now? Despairing, I turned and crawled back to the narrow staircase. I swung myself into a sitting position and started going down, sitting on each step as I descended. All I could do now was wait until morning, then try banging on the door and shouting again. Lutie had found me here years ago; maybe by some miracle she would find me again.

Of course, that was when the servants had occupied one section of the attic floor, and Lutie had come up to change her cap and apron before supper, heard some noise, and come to search for me. Now it was the middle of the night and everyone was asleep.

That is, except Miss Ingersoll. Could she possibly carry out her threat and make it look as though I had left, using my notes to verify my intentions?

Now I couldn't even remember what I'd

written in some of those attempts at explanation. I was sure they would sound incoherent. That way she could explain I was in a distraught frame of mind, which would make my going all the more plausible.

But how could she expect to get away with it? And how would she get rid of my body? I shivered at this morbid thought.

What about that carriage? Who had been in it? Was it Toby coming home from yet another late night at Woodvale Tavern? If it was, he would probably be in no condition to have noticed my weak distress signal from the cupola.

I sighed heavily and wrapped my robe more closely around me. How many hours had passed since I came up here? I wondered. It must be late. Maybe only a few hours until dawn. I could hold on until then, I told myself.

I'd heard a prisoner gets used to his cell. Something like that was happening to me. It didn't seem as cold or as frightening as it had at first. For one thing I had conquered my terrible fear of heights and gone up into the cupola; I had made the climb to save myself. I hadn't given up or given into the fear.

Suddenly I became alert, every nerve twitching. I thought I heard something. Footsteps running? I saw a crack of light.

The attic door opening? Immediately I pulled myself up and hammered on the door, yelling, "Help! Help, somebody! Please! Let me out!"

In another minute the handle of the door rattled, then the door was flung open and I threw myself forward. I was so grateful to be released, I wasn't even sure into whose arms I'd fallen. Then I heard Toby's voice: "Julie! What the hell are you doing up here?"

Sobbing with relief, I couldn't answer. Then he said more gently, "Never mind, old chum. It's all right now. Everything's all right. You're safe."

Chapter Twenty-four

The next thing I knew I was sitting on the edge of Toby's bed — sipping from a tumbler of brandy he handed me. I couldn't seem to stop shivering.

"Toby, you won't believe what I have to tell you. . . ." I said, shaking my head.

"Don't try to talk now, girl," Toby replied, "just drink up until you've got your nerves under control. And don't worry, I'm ready to believe anything after all the strange goings-on around here since we came." For once he didn't seem amused. He also seemed quite sober, as if he had not been drinking himself. At least not much. His hand was steady as it held my glass, and his eyes were very serious.

"Toby, Marshall is stealing Aunt Octavia blind," I said in a voice that shook. "And Miss Ingersoll, she tried —" I stopped as the full horror of my experience began to take hold. "Toby, she tried to kill me!"

"Kill you? What do you mean?"

"She locked me in the cupola and was going to leave me there!"

His eyes widened. "Is *that* what happened? I thought you'd gone up there to get your suitcase and accidentally got locked in. I hitched a ride home from the tavern tonight with a hack driver; he was the one who saw the light and pointed it out to me. Actually, he was telling me how his wife and lots of other people in Woodvale think Octagon House is haunted, and just then he saw that floating light and said — well, no matter what he said, it wasn't fit for a lady's ears. But when I got in the house, I just thought I'd take a look and, well, there you are — or there you were. . . ." He paused. "You say *Miss Ingersoll?*"

"Yes, Toby, it's the truth, let me tell you —" I began.

I never got to complete the sentence because just then we heard the sound of excited voices raised in agitated conversation coming from the second floor. Toby put his finger to his lips and went over to the door and opened it, then leaned out, listening. He turned back to me, saying, "It's Uncle Victor, talking with Marshall and Miss Ingersoll. Something's up. I better go see. You wait here."

Toby disappeared. I sat tense and motionless, gripping the glass of brandy. Instinctively I knew that something bad had happened.

In a matter of minutes Toby was back. He grabbed his coat, and throwing a muffler around his neck, he told me, "Aunt Octavia's had some kind of seizure. Ingersoll thinks it's a stroke. We've got to get Dr. Barret up here as fast as possible. Why Aunt Octavia didn't keep at least one horse and carriage for just this sort of emergency, I don't know." Toby grabbed his coat and flung a muffler around his neck. "I've got to run to his house unless I can flag someone passing down on the road and get a ride there."

Then he left. Shivering even more, I gulped the rest of the brandy. Soon I felt warmer, stronger. My next thought was that I had better go tell Elvira what had happened. I didn't want to be alone. And I certainly did not want to face Miss Ingersoll or Marshall.

I woke Elvira and told her about our aunt. She was awake and alert almost immediately. I could see her brain working even as she flung on her robe and twisted up her hair.

"It must be serious if Ingersoll felt she couldn't handle it without calling Jordan," was her assessment of the situation.

And she was right. Twenty minutes later Jordan arrived with Toby and went directly to Aunt Octavia's room, barely glancing in the direction of the two of us standing with Uncle Victor in the hall.

I was aware of Marshall moving like a somber shadow on the periphery of our tense little circle, but he avoided any eye contact with me. I was relieved. I hadn't yet decided what to do about what I now knew. Surely there would be time to think about it later.

Uncle Victor paced, his hands clasped behind his back, his white hair in wild disarray. At one point he turned to all of us and said sorrowfully, "I feel very guilty. I'm afraid I might have caused this — Octavia and I had a terrible argument, a most regrettable scene the other day."

Elvira's and my eyes met, and I felt Toby's quick glance. So had we all. Any one of us could have caused Aunt Octavia's attack. We had all been the source of her anger, frustration, emotional upset — all the things Jordan had warned could bring on a stroke.

I drew in my breath, and I saw Elvira's eyelids flicker faintly in her suddenly pale face, but she remained outwardly calm as she said reassuringly, "Now, Uncle Victor, no one's to blame. Aunt Octavia had high blood pressure; she has been unwell for some time. It's no one's fault. Dr. Barret told Julie it could happen at any time."

Uncle Victor just nodded, and even to us Elvira's words sounded hollow.

Just then Jordan came out from her room. I noticed his shirt collar was open and he wore no tie, that his hair was rumpled as if he had been aroused from his bed by this emergency and had not taken time to do anything but rush to his patient's bedside. He looked around at our anxious group and said brusquely, "Miss Vale has had a massive stroke. I can't tell the extent of the damage. Right now her speech seems to be impaired, and there is some paralysis on the right side. Miss Ingersoll is with her now and will remain with her the rest of the night. I'll stay for a while to see if there is any change in her condition."

Jordan was speaking in a completely professional manner, but his eyes seemed to linger questioningly on me. If he knew what I had been through, I thought — but this was not the time. How could I accuse Miss Ingersoll now, when our aunt's well-being probably depended on her skillful nursing?

"Shouldn't she be in the hospital?" Elvira asked.

A cynical smile touched Jordan's tight lips

as he replied, "Our small hospital is not very well equipped. Your aunt is better off here with the expert care Miss Ingersoll will give her. It would be foolish to put her through the trauma of moving her to a hospital where she would not receive any more attention than she will in her own bed."

"I'm sure you *and* Miss Ingersoll are doing everything possible for my sister," Uncle Victor said with his usual politeness.

At this moment Marshall stepped out of the shadows and said quietly, "I've prepared some coffee and some light refreshment, Dr. Barret, if you'd care to partake?"

Jordan acknowledged him with a brief nod. "Yes, I could do with some coffee. It may be a long night." Then he turned to me. "How are you feeling, Julie? Maybe I should take a look at your ankle while I'm here. Sit down," he ordered, and without protest I seated myself on one of the Jacobean chairs that lined the hallway.

Jordan knelt on the floor in front of me and took my foot in both his hands. At his touch I felt a breathless sensation that was the last thing in the world I wanted to feel. Our eyes met and my heart felt like melting wax within me. His fingers moved on my ankle, gently pressing where it was tender.

"Does that hurt?" he asked gently.

"A little." My voice sounded whispery.

"I'll rebandage it. It looks as though the wrapping has loosened," he said, frowning.

If you only knew, I thought, remembering the climb into the cupola.

Quickly he unwound the thick gauze bandage and expertly rewrapped it. Immediately I felt the comforting support.

"That better?" he asked crisply.

"Much," I answered. We looked at each other, but it was not the time nor place for anything else, with Uncle Victor, Toby, Elvira as our audience.

Jordan helped me to my feet as Uncle Victor suggested, "Shall we go downstairs? I suppose we can all use some sustenance."

But we had only reached the top of the stairway when we heard a shrill scream from Aunt Octavia's room. Abruptly we all halted. Miss Ingersoll came running out into the hall, sobbing hysterically.

"She's gone! Miss Octavia's dead!"

Chapter Twenty-five

The rest of the day passed in a nightmarish haze. Miss Ingersoll had succumbed to complete hysteria and had to be heavily sedated. After Jordan had seen to her, he proceeded to make a final examination of our aunt, then left. He returned later to sign the death certificate and accompany the body to the funeral parlor in the mortuary carriage.

We were all in shock and hardly a word was exchanged among us. I could not help but wonder if my cousins were burdened with the same sense of self-reproach that I was. I felt no deep sorrow at Aunt Octavia's death. I did, however, feel a sense of loss. Her influence, destructive as it had seemed, had been strong and real in my life. Her passing left a void.

We all went to our rooms, and to my own surprise, when I lay down on my bed, I slept a little. When I got up, it was late in the morning. The house seemed strangely still, filled with an unnatural silence. Outside, the winter sky had a cold sort of emptiness, a heavy grayness.

By the time I got dressed and came downstairs, I found Octagon House had become a place of formal mourning in the best traditional manner. All the draperies were drawn, and the front door was draped with a wreath and crepe ribbons. There was not a glint of daylight, but all the gas lamps were lit, and their constant hissing sound and dim, wavering illumination added to the atmosphere of melancholy.

I found Lutie had set out food on the buffet in the dining room, and the large silver samovar was filled with coffee. I helped myself and after two strong cups wandered into the drawing room where I found Toby.

Flowers and messages of condolence had begun to arrive. As the afternoon wore on, people began to call. The Vales had always been an important part of Woodvale, so the town's most influential people were among those who came to pay their respects. I could not help but think how amazed Aunt Octavia would have been to see Uncle Victor, dignified and perfectly composed, receive them. She had always underestimated her brother.

I was grateful that Miss Ingersoll kept to

her room, still under the heavy sedative Jordan had given her with the housemaid Annie posted at her bedside. I don't think I could have faced that horrible woman knowing she had tried to kill me even though no one except Toby seemed to believe that. At least now, I told myself, I had nothing more to fear from her.

By evening we three cousins were all gathered in the drawing room in a decidedly introspective mood. Whatever was on our individual minds we did not feel led to discuss. Toby had poured us all glasses of sherry, and it was Elvira who finally broke our silence by remarking, "I don't know what I can wear to the funeral. I don't own anything black. Drew hates me in black, so I never wear it."

"You have two days to shop for something appropriate," quipped Toby with lifted eyebrow. "I'm sure you'll look smashing."

Elvira gave him a withering glance.

No more was said, and soon Uncle Victor joined us. He informed us of the funeral arrangements. A service would take place at Woodvale Community Church the day after tomorrow with internment at the Hillhaven Cemetery immediately afterward.

"Ross Holden informed me that the will will be read the following day. I told him I needed to know because you three might have plans to leave. He said Octavia was very insistent that everyone concerned be present." He paused. "I hope this is agreeable?"

Without looking at each other, there was a general murmur of agreement. I think we all felt there had already been so much discussion about this will that we were embarrassed to say any more.

Uncle Victor cleared his throat, then went on. "While we are still all together, I want to assure all three of you that I have no resentment nor bear any ill will to whichever one of you Octavia named sole inheritor. I never have had any desire to shoulder the responsibility of managing the Vale estate. The main interest of my life has always been my book about the history of Woodvale and Octagon House. When it is published, that will be my reward, and in a way I will be inheriting the house. Furthermore, something a great deal more meaningful has happened. Miss Martha MacAndrews, whom you all know from the Woodvale Library, has done me the honor of accepting my proposal of marriage."

We all offered Uncle Victor our heartfelt congratulations and wished him every happiness. None of us thought it unseemly to be doing so even on the day of Aunt Octavia's death. If anyone deserved a future of loving companionship and contentment, it was Uncle Victor.

But by his announcement he had reminded us all that there was still an unrevealed mystery in Aunt Octavia's will. None of us knew if she had changed it — and if she had, in what way it had been changed.

The three of us dined alone that evening. Uncle Victor left to dine at Martha's small, cozy cottage. Afterward we all retired to our rooms.

The day of the funeral was clear and unbelievably cold. The service — structured, formal, and unemotional — was held in the ivy-covered stone church where the Vale family had dedicated two stained-glass windows and a memorial pew, into which we all solemnly filed.

I wondered, was I the only one who felt the minister's choice of scripture struck an oddly reflective note?

"Do not lay up for yourselves treasures on earth, where moth and rust destroy and where thieves break in and steal, but rather lay up for yourselves treasures in heaven — for where your treasure is, there your heart will be also."

I thought how sad it was that the last days Aunt Octavia had known on earth were totally concerned with "earthly treasures."

Afterward, the line of carriages drove out to the hillside graveyard overlooking the river, where the Vale family mausoleum of gray granite was located.

Uncle Victor, his leonine head bared to the bitter wind, stood tall and dignified with the devoted Martha beside him. We three cousins, each closed in our own thoughts, stood behind him. At a distance I caught sight of Jordan, standing alone and a little apart.

Uncle Victor went home with Martha. Elvira, Toby, and I returned to Octagon House. We cousins seemed to have little to say to one another now. It was as though we were locked into an unspoken pact of silence, waiting, as Toby had put it, for Aunt Octavia to play her final card.

I went upstairs to my room intending to finish packing, something I had put off until now. Maybe because it reminded me of the night I had been locked in the cupola and our aunt had her stroke. That night I had come back to my room and found the armoire doors standing open, the bureau drawers pulled out, my suitcase on the bed half-filled — evidence of Miss Ingersoll's plan to make it appear as if I'd fled Octagon House. I assumed she had been interrupted in her wicked scheme by the urgent ringing of Aunt Octavia's bell. When she had gone to answer it, she had found her patient in mortal stress and never returned to complete the job.

The fact that my personal belongings had been touched by hands of such murderous intent was distasteful to me. Trying not to think about it, I proceeded with my task and at first did not see the envelope propped against the mirror on the bureau. One of the part-time maids must have placed it while I was at the funeral services. It was addressed to me in Jordan's handwriting. I picked it up and held it, almost afraid to open it. I had not had a chance to really talk to Jordan since the night Aunt Octavia died.

Half-dreading what it might say, I tore open the envelope and drew out the note. "Dear Julie, With so many matters demanding my attention, I have not been able to be with you, but I assure you, you have been in my thoughts. I realize the events of the last two days may have changed things, but it is of utmost importance that we talk before you make any plans to leave Octagon House or Woodvale. If possible, could you meet me this afternoon after my office hours are over? If so, I will wait for you at the gate at five o'clock. As ever, Jordan."

My feelings about Jordan were confused. I wanted to believe in him, believe that what we had once felt for each other was possible to regain. My belief in a true, lasting love was strong. I envied Uncle Victor and meek little Martha MacAndrews their obvious mutual adoration. But there was still a cloud of mystery, uncertainty, and suspicion surrounding Jordan Barret. Could I trust him not to break my heart again?

I continued packing but intermittently checked my watch as I debated whether to meet Jordan. At quarter to five, knowing I would never be satisfied unless I gave him this chance, I decided to go.

I put on my coat, threw a scarf over my head, and hurried along the hall and down the stairs. The house, though silent, seemed to vibrate with an undercurrent of disquietude as if manifesting its inhabitants' uneasy anticipation of the reading of Aunt Octavia's will.

Heavy clouds like shredded gray cotton hovered overhead as I slipped out the side door. The wind blew wildly, tugging at my scarf and sending the short cape on my coat flapping. My ankle still hurt, and favoring it, I walked slowly down to the gate. At the bend in the drive something made me turn and look back at the house. Seeing the cupola starkly outlined against the pewter-colored sky, I shuddered. How glad I would be to be gone from here, from all my ugly memories connected with Octagon House.

Just outside the gate I saw Jordan's small enclosed buggy. He must have seen me approach and was out in a minute to help me into it. In another minute we were moving down the road out toward the countryside.

"I'd like to take you somewhere more comfortable," Jordan said, "but the proprieties, I suppose, must be observed. We'd set Woodvale tongues wagging for sure if we went somewhere in public on the day of your aunt's funeral. I didn't want to come to the house because I need to talk to you in private. There is so much I want to say . . . so much I have to explain."

I waited for him to begin.

"There are things I wasn't able to tell you before, but now that your aunt is dead — and my uncle, too — I am free to do so." He paused and I looked over at him, saw his handsome profile, the jaw set sternly, then he continued. "I didn't find out until after his death that he owed a great deal of money to your aunt. Actually, it was for my medical education." He gave a deprecatory laugh.

"Perhaps you don't know it, Julie, but country doctors are *not* very affluent." He paused, then said, "My uncle was a bachelor, with no children of his own to carry on his dreams. I became the son he never had, especially after my parents died and he became my legal guardian. He wanted to provide me with the best medical education he could, and when Miss Vale offered to lend him money, he accepted.

"Believe me, Julie, this is all as hard for me to understand as it is for you. Two years ago, when I came to take over Uncle Hugh's practice after his sudden death, things were pretty much in a mess. Uncle was not the most orderly man in the world." Jordan gave a rueful smile. "A journal he kept and in some cases personal letters were mixed in with the medical records of patients. I did the best I could to pull out what information I needed to treat people, filing the other stuff away to go through later. Then when you came back here so unexpectedly, the past was suddenly important and I decided it was time to go over them. I'm not sure why I thought there might be some clue — who knows? Fate? It was then I found out what collateral your aunt had demanded for the loan for my education. You and I were the collateral."

"What do you mean?" I asked.

Jordan continued, "I discovered some notes in Uncle Hugh's journal along with a few receipts for the payments he made to Miss Vale. In the same folder I found all the letters from you that he was supposed to forward to me at medical school. I finally put two and two together." Jordan halted, then said, "It seems your aunt enlisted Uncle Hugh's help in breaking up our romance. It must have gone against Uncle Hugh's conscience even though he complied." Jordan looked grim as he went on. "Instead of destroying them he kept them. Who knows, maybe he meant me to find them some day."

I felt bewildered. "But what about *your* letters to *me?*"

Jordan looked at me half skeptically, half sympathetically. "My dear Julie, you still don't understand that money is power, do you? According to my uncle's journal, Miss Vale bribed the Dean of Merrivale by offering her a large endowment if the college would return all letters from me addressed to you there. She told her I was an undesirable suitor who was bothering you."

"But how did Aunt Octavia find out about *us?* We were so careful. Surely Toby didn't tell her?"

Jordan shook his head. "No, it was Miss

Vale's *faithful* servant and *spy*, Marshall."

I drew a long breath. Marshall, of course; nothing much ever had escaped Marshall. That explained it.

"How cruel," I murmured. "Your uncle didn't seem the kind of person who would go along with that sort of thing —"

"Don't blame him too harshly, Julie. My medical education was the most important thing to Uncle Hugh. He told himself we were both young, we'd soon forget each other. I have to excuse him, forgive him for being weak." Again Jordan paused. "He wanted the best for me. Ironically, it was your aunt who financed my further studies in Germany and Scotland. Uncle Hugh wanted me to become a brilliant surgeon or go into research."

Jordan stopped and shook his head. "Uncle Hugh didn't plan to die so young, so suddenly. When I came to Woodvale for his funeral, your aunt confronted me with the enormous amount of money he owed her and told me that she expected *me* to repay it. She suggested that I remain here in Woodvale and become her personal physician until the debt was paid off."

He shrugged. "So, as you see, I didn't become a brilliant surgeon. Instead, I stepped into my uncle's shoes as a country doctor, indentured servant to your wealthy aunt. She also promised *me* she would leave a big endowment to our small, underequipped hospital."

I looked at Jordan appalled. This explained so much.

He tugged on the reins, and the small buggy shuddered to a stop at the side of the road. He turned toward me. "I know how all this must sound to you, Julie. But things happened so fast. Your aunt never told me she had invited you three here until right before you came — when I saw you I was stunned that my feelings for you were still so strong. But I thought you had callously gone off to school and, for whatever reason, never written. My old hurt at being rejected took over in our first meeting." Again he paused. "Then when I had a chance to think it through, it seemed that in spite of everything we'd been given a second chance. Now that the truth has come out, I have no doubts. I love you. I don't care what tomorrow's reading of the will says. I don't care if Miss Vale cut me entirely out of the will. All that matters is that you understand and believe me."

"It's a lot to take in," I said slowly.

"Yes, I know," he agreed. "Maybe it's too much. Maybe, as they say, it's too much water under the bridge. Maybe it all happened too long ago to make right." He sounded sad but resigned. "Maybe it is, after all, too late."

A long silence stretched between us. Then I spoke. "Just a little while ago, Jordan, as I was coming to meet you, I turned to look back at Octagon House, and all I wanted to do was run away and never see it again, never again feel those old haunting hurts. But now" — I hesitated before saying in a low voice — "I don't want to say good-bye."

Jordan cupped my chin and turned my face toward him. His eyes searched my face. Gently he brushed back a few strands of hair, tucking them behind my ear. Looking at me tenderly, he said quietly, "Maybe not wanting to say good-bye is another way of saying you love me?"

Chapter Twenty-six

The morning after Aunt Octavia's funeral I delayed coming downstairs until the last possible moment, not only because I dreaded the ritual reading of the will, but also because I recoiled at the thought of coming in contact with either Marshall or Miss Ingersoll, especially Miss Ingersoll.

When I came into the drawing room I saw that two rows of straight chairs had been arranged in a semicircle in front of the fireplace. Ross Holden, our aunt's lawyer, had taken a position behind a bookstand on which he had placed his portfolio.

As I entered the room, hesitating at the threshold, Elvira saw me and beckoned, and I went to a chair beside her in the row where she and Toby were seated. Her eyes swept over me critically. I knew she was probably evaluating my appearance but, noting my black dress, seemed satisfied and gave me a tight smile.

Elvira herself had managed to find something sufficiently somber to pass for mourning attire. She looked elegant in an outfit of gray bombazine elaborately trimmed with black Russian braid that becomingly set off her flaming red hair. Toby had somewhere acquired a flowing black cravat, his concession to mourning.

While Ross Holden took a great deal of time and made quite a show of putting on his silver-rimmed glasses, opening his folder, and rustling the papers it contained I glanced about me. Across from us, the staff were sedately seated in the second row — Lutie; the obsequious Marshall, who had successfully avoided me for the last two days; three scrubbed, ruddy-faced men in working clothes I assumed were the gardener and his helpers; and Aunt Octavia's part-time carriage driver.

When Miss Ingersoll entered, assisted by Annie, it was all I could do not to shudder at the sight of her. She looked dazed and haggard, and after one glance at her I averted my gaze. I did not ever want to see those hate-filled eyes again.

I was almost sure that Ingersoll, in the guise of taking her "daily constitutional," had followed the three of us to the top of the hill, concealed herself in the woods there where we were sledding and awaited her chance.

While Toby and Elvira were arguing, she must have darted out and pushed me, how else could it be explained?

The rest of the chairs were filled by well-dressed people I did not know but who were greeted by Uncle Victor and were, I guessed, some of the townspeople to whom Aunt Octavia had promised legacies either for themselves or their organizations. There was a general shifting and stirring in the room as Ross Holden signaled Marshall to close the drawing room doors, indicating he was about to begin his solemn task.

Jordan arrived, slipped into the empty seat on the end of the row next to me. As Ross Holden cleared his throat officiously, Jordan reached over and took my hand in his. It gave me an enormously comforting feeling.

"Before I read the last will and testament of Octavia Vale, I must make a statement so that there will be no misunderstanding. I am aware that Miss Vale made the remark on several recent occasions, in the presence of most of you and within the hearing of others, that she was going to change her will.

"Several times Miss Vale discussed such possible changes with me, most recently this past week prior to her untimely death. On each of these occasions we explored the advantages as well as the disadvantages of making such changes." Here Mr. Holden paused significantly. "Of course, I cannot break the code of confidentiality between lawyer and client, except to say that Miss Vale died before any of these discussed changes could be made and so the will I am about to read is the same one she had drawn up some twenty years ago."

At this Elvira shot a quick glance at me. I saw hope leap into the green depths of her eyes. "Perhaps the Vale estate was going to be divided up equally as was only fair" that spark of excitement seemed to say. Toby moved restlessly. I thought of the conversation the three of us had had at breakfast earlier and wondered if the feelings we'd express would change once the contents of Aunt Octavia's will were known.

Elvira had swept into the room with a much more cheerful attitude than the circumstances ordinarily would have warranted. She was waving a yellow telegram in her hand as she announced, "From Drew! It was delivered early this morning. Good news — a marvelous turn of events. He has had an offer from an old school friend to be the financial consultant for this man's father. We're to go for London as soon as I get home. I'm all packed and ready to go as soon as this ordeal is over." I was happy for her and amazed at how quickly she had turned from dark despair to elation.

Toby had seemed thoughtful as he stirred sugar into his coffee. "It's been a strange sort of reunion, hasn't it," he said more as a statement, than a request for our opinion. "Even the way it's turned out, I'm not sorry I came. It's given me a whole new perspective on my life."

"How do you mean, Toby?" I asked, curious.

"Well, I was angry at first at how Aunt Octavia lashed out at me. But then I realized most of what she said *was* true. I've pretty much wasted my life so far. But I finally came to the conclusion I didn't have to go through the rest of it fulfilling her opinion of me. It's like I've been given a second chance."

I started to say something encouraging, but Elvira spoke first. "Maybe Lutie's fortune-telling was right for each of us. Remember she told Toby his happiness was coming if he'd just be patient? And she told *me* a big change was coming. And it has!"

I thought of what Lutie had read in *my* coffee pounds — the circle and the crescent and an open road ahead.

"Well, one thing I know for *sure!*" Elvira said, rising from the table, a glimmer of triumph in her flashing eyes. "I'm leaving here a free woman. And once I walk out that door, I'll never set foot in this house again."

I almost dropped my coffee cup. I wondered if Elvira realized she was echoing the same words she had said so long ago?

Ross Holden's monotone voice dragged my attention back to the present as he began to read through a list of bequests to several civic and cultural organizations.

My own hand pressed Jordan's. I felt sure that whatever was in the will, it would make no real difference to us. Yesterday had been a turning point in our relationship. In Jordan's arms, I had at last known the security and love I had always longed for. Yes, surely the road ahead was opening for us. He met my eyes, and I saw in his my own glowing happiness.

Just then I caught the name Woodvale Community Hospital and listened as Mr. Holden read the large bequest that was to be administered by Dr. Jordan Barret as he saw fit. At least that was one promise Aunt Octavia had kept.

So far there had been no personal bequests, and the whole room seemed to be holding its collective breath. Ross rattled his papers and readjusted his glasses before proceeding.

"To Thomas Marshall and Lutie Hansen, my loyal employees of many years, will be administered, from the estate an annual sum commensurate with their yearly salaries, for the rest of their lives."

I was glad for Lutie, who deserved a generous legacy. I did not risk looking at Marshall to see if he felt any guilt after what he had been doing behind his employer's back. Again, I wondered to whom, and on what evidence, could I report his thievery? He would simply deny it, saying he was packing the things for safekeeping. And no one but I had seen the missing porcelain dogs, so what proof did I have? Clever as he was, Marshall had probably covered his tracks, so that nothing could be traced to him.

Ross's next words alerted me. " 'I instruct that Flora Ingersoll be given the sum of money she would have earned as a hospital nurse for the same number of years that she has been employed by the Vale family.' " At this there was a loud indignant exclamation and noisy sobs from Miss Ingersoll so intrusive that Ross Holden signaled Marshall to escort the protesting woman out of the room. Jordan leaned toward me and whispered, "I better go see if she needs another sedative; she seems quite out of control," and he left quietly.

When the stir following that outburst had calmed down, Ross Holden continued the reading. " 'And now we come to the family bequests — first, my brother Victor shall continue receiving the yearly income from the trust fund set up for him by our late parents and also lifetime tenancy of our family home, if he so desires.

" 'The family home, known as Octagon House, and the land directly surrounding it is left equally to Victor and our half brothers, Mark and Roger, or, at their deaths, to their children, Tobin and Elvira.' "

I stiffened automatically, and Elvira reached over to me with one thin hand and clutched mine. Why had neither I nor my mother been mentioned?

Was this Aunt Octavia's revenge for my refusal not to accept the sole inheritorship of the estate? But no, Ross Holden had said this was the same will she had written twenty-some years before we had all come back to the reunion. Had she been so angry at my mother for eloping that she had cut her and me forever from any inheritance?

But Ross was not finished, and I tried to focus on his next words. His voice seemed to have taken on a peculiarly high-pitched tone as he continued. " 'However, I do hereby forbid any sale of, any investments, disposition of any of the land, real or personal property of the estate to be undertaken without the advice and counsel of my lawyer and or his partners in the firm of Holden, MacKenzie, and Roberts.' "

Mr. Holden shuffled the papers for a moment, ceremoniously removed and wiped his glasses, and said, "As I told you at the beginning, this will is exactly as it was written many years ago. There is, however, a codicil Miss Vale had added, which is as follows and which I will now read.

" 'By the time this document is read, I have no fear that any scandal that might ensue will distress or disgrace anyone. Certainly I will be beyond such things. Therefore, I do publicly declare and claim that my entire inheritance along with equal share of any monies derived from sale of Vale land, timber on it, or stone quarried if the Vale quarry is reactivated, all jewelry and/or any paintings, furnishings, artifacts belonging to or bequeathed to me by my father Clement Vale, apart from what I have designated to my brother Victor, my half brothers, and their children, is to go, unless she proceeds me in death, to my natural daughter, *Clementine Madison,* or to any child or children of hers.' "

I heard a chorus of startled gasps around me.

Slowly the shocking truth of what I had heard penetrated my stunned disbelief. Aunt Octavia was *not* my aunt — she was, instead, my *grandmother!*

Chapter Twenty-seven

"At least we're still cousins!" exclaimed Elvira.

Elvira was standing at the door of my bedroom, hands on her hips, regarding me with a mixture of amusement and surprise. She was handsomely dressed in an ochre wool bouclé traveling suit trimmed with beaver and had come to say good-bye before departing for the train station.

"How I would love to be able to stay and ferret out this whole amazing story, but Toby and I have to go by Ross Holden's office to sign some papers about my — ha! — inheritance before I leave!" She walked over to the bureau and adjusted her fur Cossack chapeau in the mirror. "Who would ever have dreamed that Aunt Octavia had kept such a secret all these years?" Elvira turned around and gave me an evaluating look. "But then, someone should have guessed. You really don't look like the rest of us Vales, do you? I mean that incredible

Celtic complexion of yours and those blue eyes and dark hair must have come from some outside strain!"

I smiled with a shrug and answered, "I haven't learned the entire story myself. But I intend to. I suppose Ross Holden has all the details about who my *real* grandfather was —"

"Ross Holden!" Elvira wrinkled her nose. "Have you ever seen anyone more close-mouthed? I'm sure the government could trust him with the darkest state secrets. He wouldn't even give us the slightest hint of what the papers we're to sign contain. Everything has to be done in the exact proper manner, everything meticulously legal!" She gave a long sigh. "Ah, well, I suppose that's the best way. Then there'll be no snags or loopholes, although it will probably be months before we see a penny."

Standing in front of the bureau mirror, Elvira smoothed the fur lapels of her jacket and gave her appearance a final critical check as she said, "By the way, Toby said to tell you he'll be back to say good-bye, since his train doesn't leave until later this afternoon."

She turned around and came over to me and, putting both hands on my shoulders, gave me a little shake, saying with mock severity, "Now, you must be sure to write me all the details, promise? Drew and I will be at Claridge's in London, and I expect a letter from you very soon!"

Then she gave me an impulsive hug. "Don't let all this spoil anything for you and Jordan, Julie. True love doesn't have a price tag. He loves you whether you are a princess or a pauper. Anyone can tell that by the way he looks at you. Be happy, dear cuz!" she said in a voice that was surprisingly a bit choked. Then, in a whirl of swishing skirts and a wisp of her signature scent, she was gone.

At the sound of the carriage wheels below I went to the window and watched Elvira, escorted by Uncle Victor, sweep down the front steps in her best grande dame manner and helped into the carriage by Toby, who gave her a bow and, I felt sure, a tongue-in-cheek look. Amused, I smiled to myself, thinking how much Elvira was going to enjoy being rich.

As I stood there watching the carriage disappear down the drive, I saw Marshall hurry across the lawn toward the carriage house. I shivered. What *was* I to do about him and the things he had stolen? I would have to discuss it with Ross Holden and Jordan, I decided.

I realized I was still somewhat in a state of

shock from the will's revelations. There had been no chance as yet to get the full story. Ross Holden had assured me he would tell me everything in time.

Jordan was coming for me later in the afternoon to accompany me to the lawyer's office. Then we were to dine with Uncle Victor and Miss MacAndrews at her cottage.

Shyly Martha had offered to me let stay in her guest room until I'd made my plans. I had accepted gratefully. After all that had happened here, I did not want to spend another night under the roof of Octagon House. There was still much about my future that was uncertain.

Distracted by all the conflicting thoughts, I continued gathering my belongings and rather aimlessly packing. I was at the armoire, my back to the door, when I heard the doorknob turn. Assuming it was Toby, I called, "Come in, I'm just finishing up —" The words died on my lips as, half-turning, I saw reflected in the bureau mirror, not the figure of my cousin, but that of Flora Ingersoll.

My hands stiffened, crushing my suit jacket, my fingers suddenly numb. A kind of cold revulsion shuddered through me. "What do you want?" I asked woodenly.

Her mouth twisted sardonically, her protruding eyes abnormally bright, the pupils dilated. "What do I want? That's a good question. Only what's due me," she sneered. She took two steps into the room, closed the door, and leaned against it. I heard the lock click.

Immediately I felt sharp alarm. As she continued to stare at me with unmistakable malevolence, my apprehension became fright, starting in the pit of my stomach, rising into my throat, and prickling along my scalp. My brain telegraphed a warning — this woman was dangerous.

Instinctively I backed away from her. But she was too quick. She was beside me in a minute, grabbing my left wrist and jerking it behind me. An excrutiating pain shot up my arm and through my shoulder, and I cried out.

"Shut up, you little —" The name she called me was lost in my moan of agony as she pushed my arm higher behind my back, forcing me to my knees. "Now, you listen to me, and do as I say, or else I'll use these on your pretty face." She pressed her surgical scissors against my cheek.

There was no doubt she meant what she said. No doubt this person had tried to kill me before. The drugged brandy, the brutal attempt to send me to my death on the sled, then the poisoned sleeping powders had failed. But she was willing to try a fourth time, and this time she might succeed.

"Get up!" she ordered, dragging on the arm she still gripped. Whimpering with pain, I struggled to my feet, and she shoved me toward the little desk and thrust me into the chair. "Pick up the pen." She pushed stationery in front of me. "Write. To Whom It May Concern . . ."

My fingers shook as I dipped the pen in the inkwell and began to write.

"I, Julie Madison, renounce the designation as heir to Miss Octavia Vale's private fortune," Miss Ingersoll dictated. "I never wanted this nor will I accept it. I now appropriate it to its rightful heir, her personal nurse for twenty years, Flora Ingersoll, whose faithful, devoted service deserves to be thus rewarded."

I paused, hesitating slightly, and she gave my left arm another painful twist. "Hurry up. Get on with it." She went on dictating. "I do this with my free will and without influence or duress of any kind."

Even while my pen moved over the paper, writing the words Miss Ingersoll commanded, my mind raced. Did she mean to kill me? By what means? How could she get away with it? I could scream — then the true desperateness of my situation struck. Toby and Uncle Victor had gone with Elvira, Marshall had left as well — I was alone with this woman of mad intent in Octagon House. If I screamed no one would hear me.

"Now sign it," Miss Ingersoll directed.

"What do you expect to gain by this?" I asked as I signed my name. "Ross Holden will not accept this as a legal binding document."

"Oh, no? If you're gone or dead, he will have to, won't he? Sign it," she said viciously. With one hand still cruelly gripping my arm, she turned the paper over and blotted it. Then she pulled me to my feet. "We're going to take a little walk, miss, up to the old stone quarry."

What was in this mind obviously warped with hate and jealousy? Cold perspiration beaded my forehead. The old stone quarry! She meant to take me through the woods, up the hill to the precipice above it and then shove me into the pit! A picture of my sled smashed and broken at the bottom flashed into my mind. Now that day at the hilltop that had been clouded by the trauma that followed flashed back clearly. Vividly I remembered that as I got ready to go down on my sled, out of the corner of my eye I had seen a shadow dart out from the thick woods behind me. Then had come that thrusting shove at my back, sending my sled hurtling down the icy track toward a potentially fatal accident.

My heart sank. This time my fate was inevitable, Flora Ingersoll was very strong, probably the result of her daily "constitutionals," her rigorous health routines. She was capable of carrying out the murderous plan she had devised for me. Following it up with her plan for faking my disappearance. My body would lay broken and abandoned for days in the depths of the quarry. Even Jordan might believe that at the last minute I had panicked and run away.

All these thoughts ran through my mind in a matter of seconds. I had heard that in any life-and-death situation everything accelerates — your pulse, your heartbeat, your brain. Now I found that it was true for me. Suddenly I spotted the paperweight I had bought that day in the antique shop in Perrysville. I acted out of pure self-preservation. With my free hand I made a quick reach for it, swiftly raised it, and with all my strength flung it at Miss Ingersoll. Seeing my motion, she ducked, and instead of hitting her in the head, it struck her jaw with a smashing blow.

She let out a howl of angry pain. The assault caused her to momentarily lose her balance and loosen her hold on me. I wrenched myself free and started to run to the door. I yanked at the doorknob, forgetting she had locked the door. I lost valuable time nervously fumbling to slip back the latch. She was right on top of me, grabbing at my waist, when I finally unlocked the door and pulled it open. Wildly I pulled away from her and heard the sound of my blouse tearing as she tried to hold me back.

Gasping for breath, I rushed out into the hall and started to run. My ankle, still weak, turned, halting me for a second, but by then I had reached the stairway. Ignoring the pain, I started down, half-falling, tripping over my skirt, clutching the banister. Miss Ingersoll was right behind me, gaining on me as I stumbled down the last few steps to the second-floor landing.

Then my head snapped back. She had grabbed my hair. An arm circled my throat, and I was jerked back with tremendous force. Hairpins scattered as my hair tumbled down, but her hands never slipped. She was cursing me now, and as she yanked my head around, I could see blood was trickling down her face from where the paperweight had struck her.

Maddened with fury now, she was so concentrated on me that she did not see Lutie, who must have heard the noise from the kitchen and come to the bottom of the stairs. Wiping her hands on her apron, her rosy face startled, she looked up at us and yelled, "What in heaven's name's going on?"

I took advantage of Lutie's unexpected appearance and twisted my body in a frantic attempt to free myself, pummeling Miss Ingersoll with my right fist, my left arm hanging useless from the injury she had inflicted earlier. She was taller and stronger than I, but I kicked and screamed with all the desperation of one fighting for her life.

We struggled on the edge of the top step, then I became aware that Lutie had started up the stairs. With the last ounce of my waning strength I gave Miss Ingersoll a hard push. Thrown off-balance, she fell head-first down the steps. I saw Lutie press herself against the wall as Miss Ingersoll toppled past, her scream splitting the air.

At last she lay inert, sprawled at the foot of the stairs on the parqueted floor.

A deadly silence followed. Lutie and I seemed frozen in mute horror. As we stared at the motionless body of Miss Ingersoll, we saw a pool of blood slowly seep from underneath her in a crimson circle.

Chapter Twenty-eight

"She's dead," Lutie said in an awed tone as she looked up from her kneeling position beside Miss Ingersoll to where I sat at the top of the stairs, clinging weakly to the banister.

"She tried to kill me." I could barely get the words out.

"Her neck's broke."

"The blood?"

"Looks like she fell on her scissors. . . ." Lutie's voice trailed off, and she got heavily up from her knees. "I'll get something to cover her, and then we'll have to wait until Dr. Barret comes."

I began to sob quietly, partly from relief that I had escaped being killed, partly from spent nerves, partly from the gruesome scene before me.

I closed my eyes, not wanting to watch while Lutie spread a clean tablecloth over the crumpled body at the bottom of the staircase. I leaned my head against the wood spindle, feeling it press into my forehead.

The next thing I knew were Lutie's plump arms comfortingly around me as she led me back up to my bedroom.

Less than an hour later Jordan arrived. He had come to take me to Ross Holden's office, but when he discovered what had happened, he did what had to be done expediently. By the time he bundled me downstairs and out into his baggy to take me away from Octagon House, Miss Ingersoll's body had been removed.

Later he confirmed that she had broken her neck in the fall and punctured her spleen with the scissors clutched in her hands. She had died almost instantly.

It would take a long time for me to get over the nightmare, but Jordan's loving tenderness and the warm sympathetic care of his housekeeper, Mrs. Hammond did much to help me recover.

However, four days passed before I could gather the courage to go back to Octagon House. I wanted to see Lutie and thank her for her help on that awful day of Miss Ingersoll's attack, and also learn from her the full story behind my inheritance. Jordan went with me. We came in the back door into the kitchen, and Lutie poured us both a cup of freshly brewed coffee, then we sat down with her at the table.

"But when did it all begin?" I asked her.

"Well, Miss Julie, you can't know the times I was tempted to tell you all this." Lutie shook her head. "But, it wasn't my place. If Miss Octavia had hidden her secret so carefully all these years, who was I to break that silence? And what good would it have done anyone?" She sighed. "It all started when old Mr. Vale re-married — although of course, he was not so old then. Probably thirty-eight or forty. Of course, the second Mrs. Vale was a great deal younger, actually only a few years older than Miss Octavia, who was going on sixteen. Mr. Vale had been a widower for a long time, since Octavia and Victor were children of six and seven. So Miss Octavia was used to having her father to herself. She worshiped him and he adored her. She had all the qualities he admired: boldness of character, strength, and a fearless nature. The very things he hoped to find in his son but hadn't. Victor was a studious boy who would rather read than go riding. Octavia, on the other hand, was an excellent rider."

Lutie rolled her eyes heavenward and clucked her tongue. "And that's where Brendan Doyle comes in. Mr. Vale brought him over from Ireland to run the stables here at Octagon House. Oh, my, he was handsome — black Irish they call it. Tall, strongly built, dark, curly hair, the bluest eyes you've ever seen — well, you've got 'em yourself, so you know!" Lutie smiled at me.

"Well, of course, none of this was lost on Miss Octavia. She could hardly miss that handsome a fellow, no woman could, especially with him being around constantly. She herself was just coming into the full bloom of womanhood, a striking-looking girl, with that flaming auburn hair, eyes black and shiny as coal . . . she carried herself like a princess. And *he* couldn't miss *that!*"

Lutie paused to refill our cups, then went on thoughtfully. "But I'm not sure anything would've come of it other than just the physical attraction, because Miss Octavia was always aware of the difference in their places — she, the daughter of his employer; he, little more than a groom. She treated everyone with a sort of arrogance that didn't set well with Brendan, who had his own pride, you see. But just then, without a word to anyone, Mr. Vale brought home a bride from one of his trips back East, and it crushed Octavia. Mrs. Vale was a rare beauty, and Mr. Vale doted upon her, showering her with attention. Octavia felt she had been replaced as the apple of her father's eye, and it hurt her badly. I think it flung her into Brendan's arms — whether out of foolishness or rebellion, I couldn't say.

"The Vales didn't notice what was happening right under their noses because before long their own baby, Roger, was born and then another son, Mark. Everything revolved around this new family and their mother, making her more pampered and precious than ever." Again Lutie sighed. "I suppose Miss Octavia felt left out, neglected. Maybe it was only natural she would turn to someone who could give her the love she felt she'd lost.

"Well, the inevitable happened. When Mr. Vale discovered it, he went into a rage. He sent Brendan packing. But it was too late. Immediately plans were made to take Miss Octavia to Europe. Victor was away at school, so Mr. and Mrs. Vale, the two little boys, and Octavia left for a year. When they returned, they had a baby girl, Clementine, their new daughter, born while they were abroad — so they told everyone."

"And then everything went on as if nothing had happened?" I asked, trying to imagine the Aunt Octavia I knew as ever having experienced passion, heartbreak, and finally the ultimate sacrifice of not being able to claim her own child.

"No, I wouldn't say that. Miss Octavia returned a different person entirely. Gone was the energetic, fun-loving, adventurous young girl. Instead she seemed permanently soured by her experience. She came back arrogant, self-centered — except where Clemmy was concerned. People did remark that she was devoted to her 'little sister.' *She* was such a pretty, dainty little thing, with black curls and big blue eyes, a real doll." Lutie reached over and patted my hand. She *was* talking about *my* mother, after all. "I don't think Octavia ever forgave her father for sending Brendan away, or Brendan for taking money to leave. She never seemed to trust anyone after that."

"And no one ever found out the truth?" I asked.

Lutie shot a look at Jordan. "I believe your uncle, Dr. Hugh Barret, knew. Miss Octavia was as fond of him as anyone and confided a great deal in him. And besides, he *was* her doctor and had examined her many times." Then Lutie's face hardened. "And I suspect Miss Ingersoll discovered it. She was always sneaking around, poking her nose in where it didn't belong. You know, Miss Octavia never hid the fact that Clemmy was her favorite of father's second family. She had her pictures on display in her room, even had her baby clothes packed away. . . . Maybe, somehow, Miss Ingersoll found out who Clemmy really was, and when *you* came, Julie, looking so much like your mother, she put two and two together. That's why *you* were her target; she knew Miss Octavia was going to make you her heir."

We all fell silent, thinking of the tragic tapestry of the past. The only sound in the kitchen was the sizzle of the kettle. We had not spoken of Marshall's strange disappearance. He had not been seen since the day of the reading of the will. When Toby went to check on him in his apartment over the carriage barn, the place was completely empty. Marshall had gone without a trace. Everyone seemed bewildered by this except me. Knowing what I knew, I imagined Marshall had built up quite a little nest egg over the years, and with the annuity left to him by Aunt Octavia (I still could not think of her as *grandmother!*), he was probably comfortably fixed for the rest of his life.

Thinking of Marshall, I asked Lutie, "What will you do, Lutie, now that Uncle Victor has turned Octagon House over to the Heritage Society to use as a museum?"

"Well, I'm not quite sure, miss. I could always get a job as a pastry cook at the Stagecoach Inn — they've offered it to me before.

Then, again, I may just retire." She dimpled. "And you, miss, what are your plans?"

"Haven't you told her yet?" Jordan asked.

"What should I have told her?" I asked, feeling a blush rising into my cheeks.

"That I've asked you to stay in Woodvale and be a country doctor's wife."

Lutie clapped her hands. "That sounds like a very good idea," she declared.

We soon said good-bye and went out. The winter afternoon seemed very cold after the warm kitchen. As we stepped onto the back porch, the wind caught the small cape on my coat and whipped it over my head. Laughing, Jordan took the edges of it and tucked it back around my shoulders. Letting his hands rest there, he looked at me and said softly, "I told Lutie what I'd asked you. But you didn't say what your answer was. Have you made up your mind yet, Julie?"

I lifted my eyes and saw the longing in his. His face was ruddy in the crisp air, and he looked so strong, so stable and handsome, I felt my heart yearn to be enclosed safely in the warmth and tenderness and strength of him.

In that long moment when we searched in each other's eyes for the meaning of all that happened to us, some inner knowing told me, yes, it *was* possible — two people could be destined for each other! No matter what had separated them or for how long, they could find each other, find love, begin again. And this was Fate.

In that same moment it seemed that all Lutie's predictions for me — the opening circle of change, the crescent of happiness, the new beginning — were all possible if I said yes to Jordan's love.

"Yes, Jordan, I have. I will stay in Woodvale, and I will marry you," I answered.

Whatever else I might have said was interrupted by a kiss that was as compelling a reason for saying yes as one could imagine. A few minutes later I was cozily settled beside him in his small buggy, and we rode down the drive, through the gates, and out from under the shadow of Octagon House forever.

The employees of Thorndike Press hope you have enjoyed this Large Print book. All our Large Print titles are designed for easy reading, and all our books are made to last. Other Thorndike Press Large Print books are available at your library, through selected bookstores, or directly from us.

For information about titles, please call:

(800) 223-1244
(800) 223-6121

To share your comments, please write:

Publisher
Thorndike Press
P.O. Box 159
Thorndike, Maine 04986